For Paul Holsinger,
with all good wishes,
David D. Anderson
July 7, 1998

THE PATH IN THE SHADOW

and Other Stories of

WORLD WAR II AND KOREA

by

David D. Anderson

Cover Artist, John Askounis
Layout Editor, Wayne Spelius
Editor, Carol Spelius

LAKE SHORE PUBLISHING

373 Ramsay Road

Deerfield, Illinois, 60015

ISBN # 0-941363-44-9
copyright 1998
$12.95

For Those We Left Behind
in Tunisia, Sicily, and Italy

Acknowledgements

The earlier stories in this collection have appeared in Eyas, Artesian, La Voix, Stylus, and other journals of the forties and fifties. The later stories appear here for the first time. All the stories are based on experience that is not necessarily that of the author. All of the stories are fictions, and any resemblance to persons living or dead is coincidental.

Table of Contents

In The Immediacy Of The Events

In the Context of Life

In The Immediacy of the Events

THE PATH IN THE SHADOW

. . .Inactivity and minor patrol action marked the twenty-four hour period on the Fifth Army front south of Casino. . .

U.S. Army Communique
December, 1943

Wade walked stiffly as he left the mail jeep; he had torn the letter open and read it, eagerly at first, and then unseeingly as the words struck him. Unconsciously he pushed the letter into his breast pocket and buttoned the flap down over it. Somebody yelled something, but it didn't matter. Nothing mattered. After two years. This. Freddie getting it last night and now this. Jesus God. A Dear John. He'd heard about Dear Johns, laughed about them, sympathized with guys who got them, and now this. Only it wasn't Dear John, it was Dear Bill. Jesus Christ.

He dropped behind the wall near the C.P. and squatted on his haunches. Remembering the letter, he unbuttoned the flap, took it out of his pocket, and tore it into shreds. God damn, even the pieces still had that smell, the smell that had been on all the letters. He threw the pieces into the air; the slight breeze lifted and scattered them. They fell to the ground. He methodically buttoned the flap on his pocket and watched the pieces idly. It didn't matter. Nothing mattered, nothing except him, number one. And he was getting out.

Two years. Ain El Turk and Tunisia and Sicily and now half of Italy. Two goddamn years, a lot of good men gone in two years, and Freddie getting it last night, and it was enough. He was getting out. It was so simple. He should have seen it before, figured it out. It was so goddamn simple. No more shells, no mortars, no goddamn mud, no C rations. Hot chow and a good job behind the lines, and sooner or later, a long boat ride.

He fumbled in his pocket, pulled out a crumpled cigarette. No more patrols. Thank God. Tonight he'd ride the chow truck back. No patrol. He wouldn't mind the moon, if there was one, and the cold wouldn't be bad because it wouldn't be long, just another truck ride, this time in the right direction.

Occasionally the breeze would lift one of the pieces of paper and carry it a bit farther as he watched. Men stepped on some of them as they returned from the jeep and ground them into the mud, and it didn't make any difference. It was all over.

He noticed that some of the men looked down at him as he squatted there. They said "Hi, Bill," or "Hi, Sarge," as they passed, but it didn't matter. The word would get around that he'd gotten a Dear John, but he'd be on the way back on the chow truck. Everybody knew how long he and Freddie'd been buddies. They'd know he had to get out.

He'd better see Lipovski, the medic, while there was still time. It was so simple. All he'd have to do would be to unbuckle his combat boot and pull up his pants leg and there it was. The medic would say, "Jesus Christ, Bill, varicose veins. I never saw em so bad. You better go back." And then he'd write out a tag and there it was, so goddamn simple. He

4

flicked the cigarette away and rose to his feet. His legs did ache, bad. They had for a month, and now they were getting him out. He stepped out among the bits of paper.

"Bill! "

"Yo!" He turned. It was Hitchens, from the second squad. Big, dumb, good-natured Hitchens. "Hi kid."

"Tough about Freddie."

"Yeah, goddammit."

"Always the best guys get it. You were buddies for a long time."

"Yeah, two years almost."

"What they want to send patrols into that goddamn town for, anyway?"

"Beats me."

"Why don't they just shell hell out of it? And where's the goddamn air corps?"

"Out whoring around in Naples."

"Probably. Say, you see the lieutenant? He was looking for you."

"He didn't look very damn hard. I've been around."

He searched in his pocket for a cigarette, found a pack. He extended it. "Smoke?"

"I got some, Bill."

Wade put a cigarette between his lips, lit it. "I was just going up to see the medic."

"Legs still bad, huh?"

"Worse all the time."

"They ought to give you a ticket and send you back. Hell, I don't blame you. You been around a long time."

"Yeah, too goddamn long."

"The lieutenant was over at the C.P."

"O.K. I'll see him on the way."

"See you, Bill."

"Yeah."

Wade turned and began to retrace his steps along the wall, walking stiffly through the puddles as though they weren't there. Hitchens looked after him for a moment and then looked down at the bits of paper. He picked a piece up and looked at it. "Bitch," he said, and dropped it. Wade was just entering the C.P. when he looked up.

Always the same old smell of mold, Wade thought as he pushed the blanket aside. Moldy hay, the smell of two goddamn years of mold. The lieutenant was just putting the telephone on its hook. He looked up.

"Hi, Bill."

"You want to see me, lieutenant?"

"Yes." He grinned. "Get your mail?"

"Sure."

"Letter from Mary?"

"Yeah. Dear John."

"Oh." The grin faded. "Jesus, Bill."

"It's O.K. It doesn't matter. What the hell. Happens to anybody. You got something for me?"

"We're moving up. Tomorrow, Bill."

"Into the town."

"Yeah. At 0800. Fifteen minute artillery preparation, and then the whole battalion is moving up."

"Jesus Christ." Better tell him now. "Say, lieutenant."

"What, Bill?"

"I was just going over to see the medic."

"About Freddie's stuff? I don't know if he's gone through it yet."

"No, not about Freddie's stuff." Tell him. Tell him, for Chris' sake.

"Is that all you wanted?"

"No. There's more. A patrol, Bill. And you're my best man."

"Since Freddie got it."

"Yeah, since Freddie got it."

"Funny. He stopped by last night, like he always does, before they shoved off, and he said 'Take it easy, buddy. See you in the morning,' and they shoved off."

"You know where he was going, Bill."

"Yeah. Into the town."

"And G-2 needs the information he was supposed to get. They've got to have it by 0400, for the artillery. How many Krauts? Where? Are they dug in? Get a prisoner if you can."

"Same old story."

"It takes a good man to get a patrol in. Pick out the men you want and come back in half an hour. The captain'll be here to brief you on the map."

"O.K. Well, I better go down and see the medic."

"O.K., Bill."

Wade turned and walked out the door. The breeze took the moldy smell out of his nostrils, and a slight rain that had begun to fall while he was in the C.P. started the old jingle in his mind. Funny sunny Italy, more goddamn rain than sun. What the hell comes next? Why the hell didn't he tell the lieutenant? Well, he'd see the medic and get his tag and get out. Get on that chow truck and go down tonight. Hell with the patrol, hell with the war. With Freddie getting it, he had to get out. He slipped in the mud, swore, and went on. His legs were a little stiffer now.

He found the medic sitting on a ration case, slowly filling his bag with small square boxes. The medic looked up. Mud almost obscured the red cross on his arm.

"Afternoon, Sarge. You gettin any?"

"Yeah. All the time. I got business for you, Ski. My legs."

"Legs? Lemme look."

It was just as he had known it would be, just as easy. Ski looked at his legs after he had unbuckled his combat boots, said "Jesus, Sarge, you got it bad, varicose veins. I better send you back on the truck tonight." He pulled a tag out of his pocket, poised a pencil. "You got to have this for the doctor to see." He scribbled on it. "And for Chris' sake, don't lose it or they give us both hell." He handed the tag to Wade. Wade put it in his pocket.

"Thanks, Ski."

"Any time, Sarge." He turned back to his bag. "You won't be goin along tomorrow. Got to get this stuff ready for business. We'll miss you, boy. Take it easy."

"Yeah, you too."

Wade fingered the tag in his pocket as he turned away. The ticket. The big ticket to the free ride. The ride that Freddie could never take now. And he was going to take it tonight, the long cold truck ride in the right direction. No more patrols, no more Freddie, no more take it easy, buddy, see you in the morning, no more Dear John. Getting out for number one. The tag felt moist in his pocket. The big ticket. Better see Hitchens, tell him, then see the lieutenant.

The legs didn't ache so much now, and the stiffness was gone as he walked back along the wall, through the puddles. He avoided the C.P. and walked on through the mud, through the scraps of paper where he had squatted before. Most of them were trampled into the mud now, but a few were still clean and fresh, even with the rain on them, but they didn't matter. Funny, it didn't matter. A Dear John and it didn't make a goddamn bit of difference. Freddie had stopped and said, "Well, take it easy, buddy, see you in the morning," and now he had his ticket and he was getting out. Number one was still in one piece, not like Freddie, and he was getting out. He saw Hitchens sitting on a ration case, talking to a couple of replacements. He walked over.

"Hi Sarge," the men chorused. "Hi."

Hitchens left the group and walked a few steps to meet him.

"What did the medic say, Bill?"

"He gave me a tag. I'm to go down with the chow truck tonight."

"That's good."

"The lieutenant wants me to take out a patrol."

"That's for the birds now."

"Same patrol Freddie had, into town."

"Tell the lieutenant to kiss off. You got your ticket."

"Yeah, Freddie got his ticket, too. Last night." It was one of the new men speaking.

Hitchens turned to him. "Shut your God damned teeth." He turned back to Wade. "These goddamn kids got a lot to learn. You tell the lieutenant to jam that patrol. I'll take it. Christ."

"Never mind, Hitch. Walk on down with me."

"Sure, Bill."

"Battalion is jumping off tomorrow."

"I know." He paused a moment. "You goin down and see the lieutenant?"

"Yeah."

"Tell him I'll take it."

"I got to pick four men."

"I'll get em. You go tell him."

"O.K. Don't get any kids."

"Hell, no, no kids."

"I better get to the C.P."

"I'll get Homer and Black and a couple more."

"O.K."

They separated then, Hitchens turning toward the men who sprawled listlessly behind the wall. Wade watched them a moment and then went on toward the C.P. Hitchens was a good kid, he told himself. Learned a lot in the last six months. Make a good platoon sergeant. Good, steady, not too bright, but willing. That goddamn kid, though. Freddie got his ticket last night; that's right, one-way ticket on a one-way trip into town. The tag was damp in his pocket. He fingered it. Better see the lieutenant. And the captain. He passed the men sitting on the ration cases. They watched him but said nothing. He passed the bits of paper. Some of them were still clean. They were nothing, only scraps of paper, like the tag in his pocket. They didn't matter. Nothing did.

The blanket was over the door of the C.P.; he pushed it aside as he entered. Funny, the rain always made the smell worse. It was darker inside; he could barely make out the captain and the lieutenant. They had the map spread out on the floor and were looking at it.

"Here he is, sir." The lieutenant rose.

"Hello, sergeant."

"Hitchens is picking out some good men." Wade touched his helmet.

"Good. We've got the route for your patrol plotted. Better have a look." The lieutenant pointed to the map.

"Lieutenant?"

"Yes?"

"Hitchens wants to take the patrol."

"He's a little green yet."

The captain looked at him. "We need a good man, sergeant. This information is vital. The attack tomorrow must go through on schedule."

"Yes, sir." Wade fingered the tag in his pocket, the ticket, the one-way ticket. Tell them. Your legs. He bent over. "Let me see the route, sir."

"You cross the wall here. There's tree cover. Follow this ravine to this point." The captain traced with his finger. "Here is where last night's patrol crossed the Kraut wire. And they caught it about here, near as we can figure." He pointed a dirty fingernail.

"Yes sir." Here is where they caught it on the one-way trip. One-way trip on a one-way ticket. "I think I got it, Captain." Yeah, I got it, got the ticket. Freddie got a ticket, took a trip into town.

"You'd better get your men together and move out."

"Yes, sir."

"Too bad about Sergeant Frederick. Take care. We've got to know."

Wade turned, walked through the door. The blanket brushed across his face; it didn't matter. The smell wouldn't bother him much longer. Four men were standing near the door. He looked at them. "You ready to go?"

"Yeah, Bill." Hitchens' voice was strained. "Did you tell him I'm taking the patrol?"

"You're not taking it, Hitch."

"Jesus, Bill. What d'you mean?"

"You stay here."

"You got to go down tonight on the truck."

"I'll go down tomorrow."

"You got your ticket."

"I'll use it. Tonight or tomorrow."

"Goddammit, Bill."

"I'm taking the patrol. You stay." He turned to the men. "We better move on. Walk on down the wall, and I'll meet you soon's I pick up my stuff."

The men walked along the wall. Wade turned back to Hitchens, laid his hand on Hitchens' shoulder. "Well, take it easy, buddy. See you in the morning." He grinned and then walked on along the wall, past the bits of paper. He didn't see them; they were ground into the mud. They were nothing, only pieces of paper like the tag in his pocket, and they didn't matter.

REST CAMP

Cape Bon is a low, dark bulk that limits the bay, and that low star, no, it's a light, no, star, lone, low star, vermouth is supposed to be good for night vision, what a crock, should be more stars, should be able to see more, vermouth is wearing off, though, should be more stars, more vermouth. God, that stuff, drunk all day, lonely here, no damn people around, thank God. Why the hell thank God? Sure, God damn glad I'm alone, so what, just like on the transport, or at Bragg, I like to be alone, the only time you know what the score is, alone, no damn people around, they don't care, don't know, like the old man. Sure, son, go ahead, honor and privilege to fight, proud, what the hell did he know, others, too, got to stay away from them.

Cigarette, damn thing's damp, like the matches, tastes like sweat, everything tastes like sweat, feels like sweat, these goddamn gas impregnated OD's, why the hell can't issue us khakis, been out of the line two weeks, rear echelon have em, we get shot at, not khakis, God, prize pain, mouth tastes hot, sweet dry, need shot, cognac there, off limits, what the hell, whole damn outfit there, drunk, in bed. Get a drink there, anyway, maybe Julliene, good girl, God, what a woman, too bad, she's whore, good, like babes in that book; Christ, need khakis, cognac.

Cigarette looks funny, like tracer, arcing in air, hit wire, hanging there, no, fell to the sand, get some cognac at One-Eye's, come back, no people, maybe stay there, God, Julliene, good girl.

Long, low swells, outlined by the moon, like neon, maybe like lake, home, no, lake's dark, cold, white here, from the moon, not cold, away from the desert, but what's cold?

God damn gas flap itches, so sticky, damn OD's, water looks cool nice, swim be nice, take damn shirt off, cooler, God, I smell, can see One-Eye's lights, not so noisy tonight, door's open, what the hell. Bright lights inside, Johnson there, looking, Goddamn One-Eye looking.

"Jesus Christ, where you been, boy? That Julliene is kind of mad. She goes for you, boy."

Johnson, goddamn farmer, hell business is it of his, nosey pain all the time, One-Eye, sitting there like a Goddamn queen, peddling booze and women to the boys, bitch, and sitting there like a Goddamn one-eyed queen.

"She ver' angry, Raymon'! You have cognac, see her. She good girl."

God, she put that big, fat hand on my arm, hot, wet, feels like trench-foot."Where is she now?"

Giggle in other room, high-pitched, woman, look there. Dark, can't see much, few forms, bulb not very bright, light glistens on sweat, God, babe sounds hysterical, drunk. Goddamn giggling.

"Raymon'! "

Not in bed with Red, anyway, hear her grass sandals slapping floor, smell her, perfume, sweat.-

"Raymon', always you are mean. Why do you not come this evening, as the others? Raymon', it is you I love, and sometimes hate."

God, can taste the salt, just like the cigarette, kiss just like a cigarette, pretty good.--

16

"Mon cher, why you stay away?"

"My God, I just took a walk." Smells, sweat, like the OD's. Don't want her, like the OD's, only more.

"Red say you no like me, no like anybody."

"Get some cognac, baby, need a drink." Turn her around, pat her, loves it. "Cognac, baby."

Christ, try to get a little quiet, people gripe, Goddamn people, who the hell she think she is, at home, girls with bitchy airs, too good, whores at Fayetteville, clean, all the GI's, here, same thing, he's a GI, love him, and the Goddamn GI's eat this up. No more cigarettes, ought to tell em all to jam it, water was quiet, cool.

Sticky, can't rub off the damn sweat, shirt no good, itches, throw damn thing away, pulled a piece of skin off my lip, stings, she's coming, got bottle.

"Raymon'! You are angry. Let us sit, or there is my room. It is not so crowded, or so warm."

She's laughing at me. Bitch.

"It is silent."

Want the bottle, that's all.

"Raymon'! Speak to me."

Bitch.

"You are angry."

"No, not angry. Just fed up. Look at all the goddamn idiot GI's and all of em eating this crap up. Makes a man sick." Why do I blow up?

She's mad, steps away, her eyes.

"Oh, so you are a fool, like the others. We're not good, and you are, and then you will speak of your mother, and your so-pure sisters, like the others, and then you will want to go to bed, but we are not good, but you go."

Her tongue's stumbling. Funny.

"Shut up." Christ, I can't think. "Shut up. You make me sick." Wish I could smash her, hurt her. Woman.

"Raymon!"

She's laughing. Bitch. Get out. -- Ignore her, she's yelling, turn, get out, Fool, One-Eye watching, quiet, that Goddamn eye.

Cooler out, quiet, no sweat smell, no sick-sweet perfume, no people, nice along the beach, black, can't seem get the cork out, broke off, push the bastard in, tastes good, burns, clean taste, get it all out, want to wash in the stuff, swim, down the wrong way, good, though. God, knot in my stomach, burns.

Like an old maid, so damn touchy, so damn fouled up, why? Good cognac, knot is numb, gone. Wish to Christ I was back in the desert, such a Goddamn prima donna. She's a whore, got to act like a whore, what the hell. I asked for it, so damn nosey. Sure, went to bed with her. What's she mean, all that pure stuff, tough to be a whore. Tough, hell, half a million hard-up GI's in the country, tough hell.

Somebody yelling, bay's dark now, lots of stars, take a drink, helps eyes, closer now, like down south, the dipper, brighter than when the old man showed it to us, cleaner, used to think I could touch it, brighter now, but lots farther away.--

EXILE

It was almost evening; the sun was sinking behind the row of grime-gray buildings that lined Via Castiglione opposite the Cathedral of San Lorenzo. Long shadows were cast over the rounded stones of the street; it was the time of the evening meal, and only a few furtive figures found their way through the streets.

With the setting of the sun the chill of early April had descended on the city, and Boriso, securely warm in his OD's and field jacket, felt vaguely guilty as he caught sight of a few lone, ageless women who intermittently entered and left the cathedral. He watched for a time; in their black, shapeless dresses and shawls these gnomelike women were similar to the old women of the mill district at home. As he stood there watching, they entered the cathedral, infrequently and alone; one by one, they came out, as infrequently as they had come.

Each time the doors were opened he caught a glimpse beyond them; the occasional sight of the candles flickering on the gold of the great altar in the darkness of the interior attracted him. He stood there for a time, with his hands deep in his pockets. The warm exhilaration of the vino he had drunk earlier in the day was almost gone; he was alone, in Palermo, one of the few Gl's left in the city, and so he stood there, watching, with no place to go and nothing to do.

He wished, vaguely and uncertainly, as he watched the women enter the cathedral, that he, too, could cross the cobbled street, swing open the doors, and enter. He envied those women, because they possessed the faith that he had lost somewhere along a road lined with empty bottles and spent bodies, rumpled sheets and discarded ideas.

He looked about him; lights were beginning to emerge from the shadows of the buildings. Still, as the doors opened and closed, he could catch glimpses of candlelight on gold. He debated crossing the street and entering the cathedral, but he knew that he could not. It had been too long; the road had stretched over too many miles.

Yet he continued to stand there; he lighted a cigarette and shivered slightly in the early evening chill. People were beginning to gather in the street in front of the cathedral. There was to be a service, he thought, some solemn tribute to a long-dead saint or a reason-killed belief. He remembered other services in the past when, as a child, he had gone to church with his mother. The memory stirred willfully in his mind. He decided to cross the street and slip into the cathedral. He could stand in the rear and watch the spectacle and the people, smell the incense, and listen to the solemnly intoned music. Perhaps, for a moment, he could recapture some of that sense of belief and belonging that he had known in the past.

The few people gathered in the street had now grown to a crowd. Some of them entered the cathedral, but most of them stood there, silently waiting. He glanced at his watch; it was early, too early for a service. He decided to wait.

The crowd continued to gather; there were men as well as women in front of the church, and a great many children, who moved a little in silence. In the dusk, however, there was a sameness about the people that made them appear sexless in spite of their dress.

Then, as he watched the crowd, there was a low, resonant hum, seemingly from nowhere. It became a roar. The crowd began to move restlessly, and then erupted in sound and motion. People were shouting, straining on one another's shoulders, weeping, cheering, waving. A huge truck, its canvas cover marked with red crosses, turned the corner and came toward the crowd. Another followed, and another. They came up the street in line, more than a dozen of them. The roar of their engines dulled the noise of the crowd, and it fell silent.

The first of the trucks came to a halt in front of the church, directly across from him. He could hear the shrill protest of strained brakes as the others stopped behind it. He remembered then. It was the return of the P.O.W.'s from Africa, the Eyeties captured by the British, the wops and ginnies taken by the Americans, returned to Sicily and home.

They had signs around their camps in Tunisia, *"Riternemo."* "We shall return." They had come home, as they had promised, and as the women had prayed.

He wondered at the silence of the crowd; it was a silence of anticipation and fear. Then, as he watched, a man swung from the seat of the first truck. He raised an arm, and the motors were shut off. The crowd stood unmoving; the whimper of a child pierced the silence.

Then from the rear of the trucks, a horde of men sprang simultaneously, some of them shouting, some waving, but most of them silent, searching the crowd as they leaped down from the high backs of the trucks. The crowd broke forward, erupting again into sound and motion; they engulfed the men and the trucks. From where he stood, Boriso could see nothing but the mass that filled the street with an absorbing organism.

He felt drawn to the crowd and yet repulsed by it; in its black motion and dull roar it was torrent-like. He forced himself to look away; the roar still filled his ears, and he looked back at the mass.

The trucks began to pull out of the crowd, each in its place in line, each with its red cross dingy in the dusk; each was emitting clouds of smoke, and yet all of them together could not deaden the roar that persisted. The vehicles passed close by him; his view of the organism was lost in their bulk. The driver of one of them shouted something as he passed, but the sound of his voice was lost.

The last of the trucks passed, emitting the acrid fumes and smoke, and he saw that the mass of the crowd was dispersing; the sound of the crowd faded as its bulk decreased. Individuals appeared at the fringes; they broke away from the body. Some of them were alone, but more frequently there were small groups that walked closely and talked quietly. Some of the children were carried by tall, dark men. Others, when there was no man in the group, walked soberly, miniatures of the stolid women.

In minutes the street was almost empty. He realized that the sun had disappeared. The only light in the street was cast by the glow of the cathedral windows and the few dim lamps that threw grotesque shadows across the cobbles. A few figures remained, most of them women in black, with shawls on their heads. They entered singly, and he saw again the intermittent flicker of candlelight on gold. He watched for a moment and then turned away. He put a cigarette in his mouth but neglected to light it as he walked the long road. The end was not in sight, he knew, and yet he had to go on. There was no return for him.

THE FRUIT OF THE TREE

Sun and sea and cliff and men; GI's, two of them, walking out of the sun into the shadow along the road, looking ahead at brown-white buildings against the blue sea and bluer sky in June, 1944. Defenders of democracy, America's emissaries of good will; combat infantrymen, experts with M-1, bayonet, grenades, chewn gum. The liberators. Heroes of the patriot and the prostitute. American soldiers with a three-day pass in their pockets, pausing in the shadow of the overhanging lava accumulation of a thousand years.

"There it is, boy. Torre Annunziata. Put a roof on it and it'd be the biggest cathouse in the world."

"That's what they say, Red."

"And you and me are really goin to have ourselves a time, kid."

"On the strength of competent medical advice, Corporals Hansen and Black advance on the town to do what comes naturally."

"That's for goddamn sure. Well, we better get movin!"

"Yeah, let's get moving."

"Christ, it's been a long walk."

"Too damned long. It better be good."

"Listen, boy, when I say something is good, it's good. I tell you, I'm a connoisseur of the stuff."

"It's been a long time for me."

"Not for me. A connoisseur of the stuff can find it even up on the line. Did I ever tell you about the time. . . ?"

"Yeah, you told me. In the hospital."

"I guess. After the doctor gave me the passes and told me we should take off."

"Just what did he say, Red?"

"Well, he says, 'Why don't you go out and get good and stinking drunk and get laid before you go back up to your outfit.' he says, 'and take that kid Black with you.' "

"Why did he mention me?"

"Guess he figured you needed it."

"Well, we're not drunk yet."

"Give us time, boy, give us time."

"I've never been really drunk, except that one time in Santa Maria. I was pretty drunk then."

"You stick with me, kid, and you'll learn. You're with an artist."

"That time in Santa Maria was pretty bad. I fell out of the truck and could hardly walk for a week."

"Yeah, I remember. Just before you came to the outfit. Hell, when you went limping on that patrol I didn't know what to do with you."

"You told me to stick with you."

"Boy, you did. Funny, when you made corporal and transferred out, we both get hit."

"Yeah, funny. Red?"

"What?"

"We may as well crack that bottle."

"Yeah, may as well. This goddamn ginnie dust is in chunks in my mouth."

24

"Mine, too." "Red?"

"Yeah, kid?"

"What if we get dosed?"

"Hell, you know what the man said. If you can't leave 'em alone, take a pro."

"Yeah."

Two men in uniform, beads of sweat on brown faces. Two men sprawled on the shoulder of the road in the shadow of the overhanging cliff, blue canvas Red Cross bags beside them and the black macadam stretching out behind them, reaching for Castellemare, falling into the sea after a quarter mile in the white sun. Capri jutting lazily out of the bluegreen sea, a monstrous haze-black cat at the end of the road, patiently awaiting the return of the mouse-men.

"Got the bottle open yet, Red?"

"I broke the cork off. Push it in." He handed the bottle to Black.

"Is this stuff greenish, Red, or is it my eyes?"

"You been watchin the sea too much, kid. That stuff's red as hell."

Black tipped the bottle, swallowed twice in close succession, and handed it back to Red. He spat out a bit of cork and wiped his mouth.

"Good stuff."

"Ought to be, for two hundred lire. When we first hit this country, I could've bought half of Brindisi for that." He tipped the bottle.

"We should've got another one, Red."

"The stuff gets too warm, carrying it in the sun." He passed the bottle back to Black. "Well, kid, shall we hit the road?"

"Hell, Red, we've got three days. And it's kind of nice, sitting here. You can almost make out Ischia on the horizon, but it's a little too hazy."

"Three days is a long time on the line, but hell, not here. Be gone before you know it."

"I suppose."

"What's the matter, kid?"

"Nothing. Maybe we should've gone to Capri."

"Be just another rest camp. You want to see Italy, don't you?"

"Yeah, I want to see Italy."

"You stick with me. Torre Annunziata is a good beginning. Then we'll go up to Napoli."

"See Naples and die."

"What dayah mean by that?"

"Somebody said that once."

"Must have been one of the brass. We may as well finish the bottle."

"Save us carryin' it."

"Yeah."

Black tipped it again and let the vino run down his throat. A bit of the stuff escaped and riveleted down the corner of his mouth. He handed the bottle to Red and wiped his mouth with the back of his hand.

"It would look like hell, two non-coms carrying a bottle around and taking a nip now and then, wouldn't it, Red?"

"Yeah. Bad example." He laughed. "Especially in a cathouse town." He lifted the bottle. "Well, here's to hell."

"Save me a swallow."

Red took the bottle away from his lips. "Sorry, kid. You should've spoke up sooner." He threw the bottle in the direction of the sea. It disappeared silently beyond the edge of the road. Black listened expectantly for a crash. None came.

"Red?"

"Yeah, kid?"

"You know, I've never been laid."

"Jesus, kid. Well, we'll fix that. You got a treat comin'. Let's get this show on the road."

"Okay, Red."

Torre Annunziata. City by the sea. Night's white jewel on the bay of Naples. City of pleasure, city of sin, spawner of Al Capone, spreader of the Old Joe. Good town to get drunk in, with the sixteenth century fountain in the square and a pro station in its shadow. Life in a circle in the city by the sea. Pimp barber pimp. Pimp whore pimp. Put a roof on it and you'd have the biggest cathouse in the world. Torre Annunziata. Two GI's, a bottle, a seaside cafe, spent genitals, silence.

Why so quiet, kid?"

"Remember what the chaplain said?"

"How the hell would I know?"

"He said Italy was the most moral of countries."

"That's a crock."

"He said that GI boots are trodding on its ruins."

'That, too, is a great big smelly crock."

"I don't know, Red. Something's wrong."

"Sure. The chaplain."

"Nothing wrong with this place. It's quiet, it's cool, you can hear the sea, and you can hear the kids singing *Oh, Marie.*"

"Yeah. And drink cheap vino and get plastered and go out and shack with some lousy whore." He pounded on the table. "I wish that ginnie bastard would bring another jug."

"Nothing wrong here, and then you walk outside into the sun, and those same kids are a bunch of grinning little pimps."

"What's the matter with you, Black? I thought you were a good man."

"There's nothing wrong with me, Red."

"Leg still bother you?"

"No."

"Didn't you get your money's worth from that ginnie whore?"

"I guess."

"Want to take a walk down the street?"

"Not now."

"We'll get a bottle and some babes and go out on the beach this evenin"

"Red?"

"What?"

"What's it like if you get a dose?"

"Ever have a bad cold?"

"Like that?"

"Yeah, like that."

"Wish he'd hurry up with that bottle."

"Here he comes. Christ."

"I don't feel drunk, Red."

"You will." He leaned back in his chair and took the bottle from the man's hand. "Here. You pour. Like non-coms and gentlemen by an act of the local board."

"Red, I can't get drunk." He handed the bottle to Red.

"What's the matter? You sick or somethin'?"

"No."

"Then what the hell's the matter?"

"It's my leg, Red."

"Your leg? Want me to have a look?"

"No. Maybe I better go back to the hospital."

"Maybe. Want me to go along?"

"No. You stay here, Red."

"I better go along."

"No, I can get a ride, maybe."

"Well, I oughtta go."

"There's only three days, Red."

"Yeah. That's right. Three days. Two and a half now."

"Well, I'm going to go, Red."

"So long, kid. Take it easy."

"Sure."

Black pushed his chair back from the table and walked out into the late afternoon sun. Red watched him casually and then poured himself a drink. "The little bastard," he said to himself. He picked up his glass and drained it. "The little bastard. He's got a lot to learn." He placed his glass down on the table and picked up the bottle.

ITALIAN INTERLUDE

The water in the canal was green and stagnant in the bright, hot sunlight, but to the two dirty men in sweat-streaked OD's and field jackets, it was cool and quiet as they huddled in the bushes by its edge. Both of them were bareheaded and beads of perspiration made streaks in the heavy grime of their faces. They sat there for a long time with their heads in their hands, their bloodshot eyes half closed.

Then one of them, obviously the younger, spoke in a strained monotone. "What are we going to do, Cole? They've probably written the whole patrol off now."

The other, a lank, sandy-haired man of about thirty, removed a blade of grass from between his teeth and spat. "That lousy, stupid, goddamn ninety-day blunder should have known better than to try to penetrate this Kraut set-up with seven men. I hope to Christ he's dead."

"Hansen is, Cole. I saw him get it in the guts. He just laid there." The boy shuddered. "God, he was a mess."

"Cut it out, kid. Hansen's better off than we are, I reckon. If that goddamn Parsons is still alive, I'm going to get him myself. Four good men gone, and we will be if we don't get out this mess."

"How far back is it, Cole?"

"I don't know, kid. We must've covered ten miles last night, getting away. Christ, I don't even know if we're still in Italy."

"Jesus, what can we do, Cole?"

"All I can figure is follow this canal. It's part of old Mussolini's setup for those farms we saw. It should hit the beachhead perimeter somewhere south of Nettuno."

"What was that?" The boy looked up. "Jesus, a bird. I thought it was a Kraut."

"Jumpy, kid?"

"And how!"

"So am I. I wonder if we should try to now or wait for dark."

"It's a long time to wait."

"Yeah. Let's get going. You take my forty-five, and I'll tote the M-1." They exchanged the weapons.

"Thanks, Cole. I'm just about pooped."

The two men half-slid, half-scrambled down the short bank to the canal's edge, and Cole in the lead started to creep through the swamp grass and rushes. The boy followed silently, ten or twelve feet to the rear.

It was long and hard and wearing, crawling through the swamp grass in the hot sun, and the stench of the canal mixed with the smell of the sweat-stained clothes as they rested, frequently and silently. The large, persistent green flies buzzed tirelessly and effortlessly in the stifling heat and stench. The routine grew endless; crawl, creep, rest, walk, rest, creep, and fear grew in them as time seemed to have stopped.

The boy was frightened as he had never been before, even more than he had been that first clear, cold night in combat in the mountains. Only a month ago, two months? Christ. Then he had been afraid of the dark and the sudden noise and the long silence. Then it was winter, with hate and fear and cold and the high hills, black and wet and eternal. Now it was spring, and day, and white sunlight, and the earth and sky and water were bright, and the mountains, purple-hazed, were friendly and warm.

And he was afraid of so many things, life and fear and silence, and he wondered if he were nineteen and alive or ninety and dead, and what difference did it make? And he wondered where they were going, to Nettuno or hell, and why, and he knew that he cared, but that was all. He shivered in the heat and the stench, and he continued to creep, watching Cole, brown-backed in the green of the rushes.

Cole was afraid, too, but he was more angry than frightened, and he swore as he crept, he cursed his knees, sore from the grind of gravel, and the monotony made a pattern in his mind . . .sonova . . . bitch . . . sonova . . . bitch. And then it faded, as he went through the moist grass and rushes and occasional clump of bushes. He watched the bank and the water in front of him, and he wondered and worried about the absence of life in the greenness ahead, and he hated the war, Italy, his knees, and the lieutenant and the Krauts and life, and the drive and fear that made men go on.

The boy watched Cole, and crept when Cole crept and rested when Cole rested, and the day went on and on, in the silence of the rustling grass, and he thought of people and the past, and the clear image of the iron rail along the walk at the beach at home, and he knew that if he could think and remember, he could go on, and then the bushes on the bank were shaking, and he stopped. A head protruded, a blond boy's head, wearing a long-peaked Kraut field cap. The head turned and saw Cole, and the boy wanted to shout, to warn Cole, but he could not. Then the forty-five was in his hand, and he fired wildly, blindly.

The blond hair on the back of the head turned red and white and gray, and the cap, crimson, flew from his head. It seemed to hang for a moment in air, and the head poised on the bank, and then the cap fell, and the head, with a near-naked brown body, tumbled down through the bushes and over the bank. It sprawled half-in, half-out of the green water and lay still as wide circles spread out across the canal.

The boy watched, horrified and uncomprehending, as Cole whirled, rifle ready. He stood up, looked at the Kraut, and said, "Thanks, kid." He looked at the boy, walked back, and slapped his shoulder. "Good work, kid. Let's move, fast." He stepped over the legs of the German, paused, and looked down. He spat, said, "Kraut bastard," and went on.

The boy followed, and they crept more rapidly through the brushes. Then the boy looked back, and he saw the German with the blond, red, white, gray hair lying sprawled half-in, half-out of the green, stagnant water, and he saw the flies circle and light, and the sun was bright in the sky.

THE LONG, CLEAR VIEW

Lieutenant Walker wasn't drunk, although he had expected that he would be and knew that he should be, after drinking a quart of the *vino rosa* and starting on the second. He knew, though, that if he did keep on drinking the stuff, alone, and as rapidly as he had been doing since he came into the officers' club, he would be before the evening was very far advanced. And, what's more, he didn't give a good God damn. The whole rotten set-up made him so damn mad that he could hardly see straight. He poured another glass of the red wine and stared at it for a moment.

The music was getting on his nerves. The Italian string orchestra with its stepped up, meaningless and feelingless version of American jazz bothered him more than the people who sat around the dingy room, the officers in sun tans, wearing the Fifth Army patch on their freshly-starched shirts, drinking rapidly, and talking more rapidly to the civilian girls with dark hair and darker eyes who sat with them. He could ignore them, all of them. Neither they nor their world existed for him, but the music was deadening in the impact of its artificiality.

He picked up the glass; the gritty sediment that sank slowly to the bottom stood out sharply against the light from the orchestra platform. It was all so goddamn stupid, he told himself, the whole rotten system. He had felt his disgust grow in him all afternoon. It had started before they had left the bivouac, and all during the jeep ride into town, he had known that it was no use, that Rome, or any place in the backwash of the war, held nothing for him. Shideler had seen it, he knew, but had said nothing; he had understood. Shideler was a good non-com and better friend. There was no need for words between them. They had been together for a long time. That's what made it easier for both of them so much of the time, and that's what made it harder at other times, like at the hotel, when they had stopped for billeting that afternoon.

After they had noted the sign that it had been taken over as a transient billet, they had stopped, and, while Shideler was locking the jeep, he had gone in. There was a PFC with thick glasses behind the ornate desk; he stiffened perceptibly and straightened his tie as Walker approached.

"Good afternoon, sir." The man spoke with an affected Ivy League accent. Walker thought of the Cornell Hotel School; he remembered it vaguely.

"Do you have room for two?"

"Certainly, sir. You'll have to register." The clerk laid two of the yellow billet requisition forms on the desk. "I'm afraid you'll have to share a room."

"That's all right. We've been living together for quite a while."

"Line outfit, sir?"

"Yes." Walker picked up the pen from the desk and wrote his own name hurriedly, and then scrawled Shideler's on the other blank. The man watched his movements with his eyes and then picked up the papers.

"You'll have to add rank and serial numbers, sir. For the record, you know."

"All right." He wrote Lt., 0-1873156 behind his own name, and then added staff sergeant to Shideler's. "I don't know the other serial number. He'll have to fill it in when he comes in."

''That's all right, sir." He glanced at the papers. "Oh, sir, I thought you knew. This billet is for officers only. They haven't requisitioned any places for the enlisted men yet."

"What? "

"The sergeant will have to go elsewhere. Regulations, sir."

"Regulations, hell. He's my platoon sergeant."

"I'm sorry, sir."

"You're sorry?" Walker turned on his heel and walked out the door. Shideler had just climbed out of the jeep. He waved at Walker.

"I can't find the chain to lock this damned thing."

"That's all right. We're not staying."

"What's the matter? They full up?"

"No. Officers only."

"Well, hell, you can stay."

"They can shove it, for all I care. God damned rear echelon regulations."

"It's all right, sir. A guy gave me an address, and I can go there and shack up."

"No. The hell with this noise."

"I'd just as soon shack up, lieutenant."

"It makes me so goddamn mad."

"Me, too, but what the hell. Nothing you can do about it."

"I know."

"Well, I'll go look up this babe. You go back in and get a room. Maybe they got hot and cold running WACs."

"I don't like it. We came to town together."

"It's all right, sir. We just forgot."

"Yeah, I guess we did."

Yeah, we sure did, Walker was thinking as he sat alone, drinking in the officer's club. We sure forgot about all the regulations and red tape and niceties of military protocol. We forgot a lot because we were too damned busy to remember. These bastards around here, with their freshly-laundered sun-tans and steady shackups don't forget. They remember the line. They draw the line and they make damn certain that nobody steps over that line, because they're afraid. They want to hang on to what they've got, and they're afraid of the Shideler's. He drank the glass of vino rosa and poured another. Looking up, he noticed that the place was getting crowded. The music was muted by the laughter, the sound of shuffling feet, the drone of conversation.

The sons of bitches, he thought to himself. The sons of bitches. Laugh. Sing. Live on the fat of the land. You never had it so good because of that goddamned line you've drawn. You got your first square meal and your first pair of shoes in the army. You never had it so good, any of you. He picked up his glass again, tasted the vino, and felt the thin warmth of the stuff. He has beginning to sweat as he put the glass back on the table. He felt like smashing it, like throwing it, like shouting, like swearing. Instead, he reached for the bottle and noticed that it was almost empty. The sweat began to creep down his temples. He brushed it away with his sleeve and looked around for a waiter.

The smoke bothered his eyes; it was like a fog hanging over the place, diffusing the lights, and making the forms in the room vague and ill-defined. He felt like vomiting, and then the feeling passed. He poured what remained in the bottle into his glass. It wasn't much. He would drink it and then go out; find someplace else, someplace less confining, or he would go to bed, or he would find a woman. It didn't matter. A woman. He hadn't had a woman in a long time. A month. Six months. That's what he needed, a woman. Everybody had a woman. He fumbled for a cigarette. The pack was empty, and he threw it in the middle of the table. He wanted a cigarette, a cigarette and a woman.

A close soprano voice interrupted his thoughts "I wonder if we might share your table, lieutenant? The club is so crowded."

He looked up. Two women were standing there, in uniform. He could see the serpents entwined about the staffs on their lapels. Nurses. Shiny second lieutenant's bars glinted in the murky atmosphere.

"No, I don't mind. Sit down." He picked up his glass. He could ignore them. Women in uniform. Goddamn phonies. He remembered the bad joke about full blouse pockets and women in uniform and grinned a little. He looked up self-consciously.

"Some secret joke, lieutenant?" The one who had addressed him before was speaking.

"No, not a secret joke. An old one. You've heard it." Christ, he told himself. Not a conversation. Ignore them. The hell with them. The hell with talking, the hell with words.

"I hope we're not intruding, lieutenant."

"No."

"Are you meeting someone, lieutenant?"

"No." For Christ's sake, why doesn't she shut up and knock off that lieutenant stuff?

"I'm meeting my boy friend. I shouldn't call him that, I suppose. I just met him." She smiled self-consciously showing too-white teeth. "He's a major attached to G-2."

"How nice."

"We've just been in Italy a week. We landed in Naples last Monday."

"I trust you're enjoying yourself."

"It is interesting."

"Yeah, I know." Why doesn't she shut up? At least the other one has brains enough to.

"Are you stationed in Rome?"

"North, a ways." Yeah, quite a ways.

"Oh, that looks like him at the bar. Excuse me?"

"Sure." Goddamn right, I'll excuse you. Jesus Christ. Excuse you for living. He ignored her as she rose; picked up his glass and drained it. He beckoned to a passing waiter, and then stared at his glass. He couldn't hear the music any more. Maybe they weren't playing. Maybe it was just the noise drowning them out. Anyway, good. He could ignore the rest, but not that phony jazz. His head was clearer. Maybe it was because there wasn't any more music. His stomach was steadier, too, and he knew that he could drink all night without getting drunk. It had been a long time since he felt like that. The other nurse was still at the table, but he couldn't even feel her presence. Thank God she had sense enough to keep her mouth shut. Maybe she would go away, go join her friend, go find a shack up.

The waiter placed a bottle on the table and handed Walker a pencil. Unconsciously he scrawled his name on the slip and waved the man away. He poured a glass full of the *vino* and raised it to his lips. The waiter returned and placed a glass in front of the woman. Walker ignored the action, ignored the nurse as she filled her glass from the bottle. Hell with her, plenty more where that came from. Hell with all of them. He looked up.

She was watching him, staring at him like he was a goddamn freak, or something under a microscope. She was toying with her glass and watching him.

"I'm sorry if we intruded, lieutenant. Lucille just doesn't think."

"It's all right." He noticed the thin lips, tightly clenched except when she spoke.

"You want to be alone." It was a statement. "I'm sorry."

"I said it was all right." He noticed her breasts. They were full under the confines of her tight blouse. Suddenly he wanted to touch them. She bit her lip and looked down at her glass. He looked away and then back at her. She was breathing deeply; the strain was obvious. She should either unbutton the damn thing or get a new tailor, he thought.

"I'll go away." She looked up from her glass.

"No. I don't want you to."

She picked up her glass and sipped the *vino rosa*, looking at him over the top of her glass. It bothered him again. She seemed to be studying him. He should have let her go. Hell with her. Leave her sit here. He picked up his own glass and drank all of the vino rapidly. It went down easily, warmly, and he felt good. He stood up.

"I'm going to take a walk."

She put down her glass. "Don't leave. I feel that I'm chasing you away. And I hate to sit here on exhibition, alone." She looked apologetic, as if she had said more than she had intended to, as she watched him, not staring any more. He felt momentarily guilty.

"I won't talk any more. I know you don't want to."

"Hell. I said it was all right. I'm going to take a walk. You can come along, if you like." If you don't like, the hell with you, he thought. This town is lousy with stuff, all kinds, if I want it. The hell with you female GI phonies. He pushed his chair under the table.

"Wait."

"If you're coming, come on."

"All right." She looked around the room. "I don't see Lucille."

"The hell with her." He looked at her breasts again. She was breathing deeply. The tightness of her blouse made them seem large. Larger than they were, he thought, larger than any woman's had a right to be.

She stood up then, hanging her long-strapped bag over her shoulder. He walked to the door, threading his way through the closely-spaced tables, and she followed, trying to match his long strides. He could feel the nearness of her, see the largeness of her breasts in his mind. A woman. That's all. A woman. That's what he wanted. That's what he was going to get, and she knew it. She wanted it. They all did. That's what they hang around for, but they never admit it. Never. They're all virgins, all of them, till they die. All of them, every goddamned one, even if they're married for forty years.

They reached the door, and the coolness of the night air struck him momentarily. He turned to her. She was smaller than the uniform made her appear.

"I'm just going to walk. You can go back if you want to."

"I'll walk, too. It was so stuffy in there."

"All right."

"If you want me."

"Yes." Jesus. If he wants her. Women. What did she think he wanted? The rebels in the outfit had a name for it. Poon tang. That's all. No strings, no red tape, connected with it. Plain, everyday poon tang. That's what they called it, and that's what it was. See some woman you want, and take her. No formalities, no money, no mumbled words, no hard feelings. It's so goddamned simple that way. See what you want and take it.

"You're from a combat outfit, aren't you, lieutenant?"

"Yeah."

"Infantry?"

"No. Engineers." Christ, her breasts. Even in the dark I can feel them.

"And you're married."

"I don't know."

"I noticed the ring."

"I still don't know. I don't know anything any more. What difference does it make?" He turned to her, grasped her by the shoulders, kissed her viciously. Her lips were too thin; it wasn't a good kiss. She didn't say anything; he didn't expect her to, and he pulled her closer and dropped his hand to her breast. It was full and round, larger than his hand, but it seemed inanimate; like a soft stone, or a rubber ball, he thought. He couldn't see her expression in the darkness, and it didn't matter. All women looked alike when they got worked up. He kissed her again. She pushed him away with a surprising strength.

"Don't. Please don't."

"Why not?"

"Because we don't have any right to."

"Right to?"

"No. We have no right to."

"What do you mean, right to? It doesn't make any difference."

"You know what I mean. We won't stop with this."

"Come on." Jesus Christ. It was all the same. Why the hell can't they be honest with themselves? Who the hell are they trying to kid? He placed his hand on her breast again. She was breathing harder, but still it seemed inanimate, sexless. She pushed at his hand. He let it drop. The goddamn lying phony.

"What's the matter with you?"

"There's nothing the matter. Only this isn't fair."

"Why isn't it? What else is there?"

"That isn't the point. This isn't right."

"God, you talk like a tract."

"I don't care. I just can't."

"You like it and I like it. What else makes it right?"

"Lots more. There are such things as conventions."

"My name is Henry; what's yours? How do you do?"

"I didn't mean that. An hour ago I didn't know you existed. And now all you can think of is expending yourself."

"My, what a nice way to put it."

"You don't have to be bitter."

"Bitter, hell. Tell me, Florence Nightingale, just what the hell did you expect when you came over here?"

"I didn't expect things like this. I do have a good Midwestern conscience."

"You mean a fear complex."

"There is such a thing as wrong."

"What is wrong?"

"Relations like this are wrong."

"You're a big girl. You should understand. There is no wrong. There's bad and there's good, but no right and wrong."

"There's no distinction. You can use any names you like. That doesn't change the facts."

"If you like things, they're good. If you don't, they're bad."

"Life isn't as easy as that."

"You're mistaken there, honey. You and a lot of goddamned people. Life is as easy as that. That's where your Midwestern conscience plays tricks on you. You think that if something is easy, or if the you like it, it's wrong. It has to be complicated and mixed up and full of the accumulation of five thousand years of crap. That makes it automatically right. Otherwise, you're afraid." He put his hand on her breast again.

"Don't," she said again.

He stepped away from her. "All right. If that's the way you want it." He was sweating again, and he wiped his face with his sleeve.

"Where are you going?"

"What difference does it make? You go back to Lucille. She'll find you some nice major from G-2, and you can call him your boy friend." He turned away and began to walk rapidly down the dark street. He felt like a bastard, and he wanted a drink. Maybe he could get drunk tonight, after all.

THE BURDEN OF PROOF

Colonel Scott, my defense counsel, entered my plea of "Not Guilty," and we sat down. The prescribed ritual for dispensing military justice went on. Twenty years in the army had familiarized me with most of the roles: I had been court martial officer, trial counsel, defense counsel, witness, but this time was different. My part was a new one, difficult to play, even more difficult to believe. I was the accused.

I looked down at the smudged carbon of the charge sheet on the table in front of me. I didn't read it; I didn't have to. I knew the charges, the specifications, the witnesses, the accuser. At least they had been made known to me. The government had been careful in safeguarding, explaining, and interpreting my rights, and Scott had been just as concerned. I could, if I chose, simply sit there without speaking or moving until the trial was over. The burden of proof was on the government.

Scott shuffled his feet then; I looked up from the onion-skin paper. Around me, the court martial board, the prosecution staff, and the carefully selected audience were settling into their parts. The trial counsel, a colonel from the Adjutant General's Department, rifled his notes and then stepped in front of the board. I looked down again. I didn't want to listen. I knew what was next in the ritual: the prologue to a long, tedious drama that could be expressed in a sentence. I was a traitor.

My mind was instinctively formulating a prayer or a plea for acquittal, but I knew that was useless. In the letter of the law I was guilty. If there was a question of that, I wouldn't stand trial. The facts were established long before this hot

August morning. Military justice is interested only in facts, in black or white, and the facts in my case were undoubtedly black. My not guilty plea was in effect a farce, but I determined to play my part as best I knew how. My role required that plea.

I heard a door open and looked up. A witness, a young sergeant, came into the room. I looked down again at my folded hands in my lap as I had seen countless guilty men do. The ritual did not demand that I listen, and there was no need to. I was a traitor; while a prisoner of war, I had aided, abetted, and given support to the enemy. I would sit there as required, I would accept my punishment, and after that, only God knew. I had no right to go home to my wife, and I couldn't go on living with myself.

For months I had been trying to think back and reexamine those dark, unreal years as a prisoner, but somehow I couldn't. It was like looking through the translucent paper window of a Japanese house. There was the play of vague shadow on the screen and that was all. I couldn't remember. The only explanation was my guilt; the sheer horror of my realization of it had driven it deep in my mind. The rumors that I'd heard in the months since Panmunjon and my arrest and the presentation of the charges didn't permit any doubt. I was guilty. I had betrayed the oath I'd taken twenty years before. But I didn't know why.

Scott nudged me suddenly. As I looked up, he inclined his head toward the witness chair. Reluctantly I looked over. The little sergeant sat forward on the edge of the chair and stared straight ahead, repeating his name, grade, and serial number in a rapid monotone in answer to the trial counsel's question-phrased order. As he finished he glanced in my direction and wet his lips; then, folding his hands in his lap, he settled back in the chair and looked up at the trial counsel standing easily in front of him.

"Sergeant Hopkins, do you know the accused?"

The little man cleared his throat. "I do, Sir."

"Do you see him in this room?"

"I do, Sir." His voice was almost inaudible; I had to lean forward in order to catch his words.

"Will you point to him and state his name if you know it?"

I sat back in my chair, tensely conscious of a hundred eyes, and stared back at the little sergeant. I remembered him then. Of course he knew me. How could he help it? Why did they have to be so melodramatically correct? I'd never realized the absurdity of it before. The sergeant's eyes wavered and he lifted his hand.

"There he is, Sir," he said, pointing.

"Do you know his name?"

"Colonel Waverly, Sir."

"Thank you. Can you tell us, Sergeant, how you are acquainted with the accused?"

"I was his driver, Sir. In Japan and Korea." His voice dropped almost to a whisper and I leaned forward in my chair again. The hundred eyes moved to the sergeant.

"When was that, Sergeant?"

"From June to December in 1950."

"What is the significance of the latter date?"

"Sir?"

"What happened to break that relationship in December?"
"I. . .we was captured, Sir." He wet his lips again.

"By the Chinese Reds?"

"Yes, Sir."

"Can you tell us, in your own words, what transpired on the day that you were captured, Sergeant?"

"It was Christmas day, Sir. We was going back to the regiment from division."

"How long had you been absent from your regiment?"

"About. . .six hours, I guess."

"And you were returning. Was your regiment in combat at the time, Sergeant?"

"Yes, Sir."

"Do you know the nature of your business at division headquarters?"

Colonel Scott, my defense counsel, shuffled his feet. As I looked at him, his lips formed the word objection. I shook my head. Let Sergeant Hopkins speak out if he knew. It didn't matter. We had gone back to division so that I could go to Mass. Midnight Mass in a squad tent on a ten-below zero Christmas Eve while hordes of Chinese poured toward us through the snow.

I don't know why I wanted to go; it was a whim. I am not a Catholic and am normally non-religious, but the regiment was secure and the chaplain had invited me that afternoon, so I went. And after standing and kneeling for an interminable hour in the cold, I was reluctant to start back immediately to the regiment. We caught two hours' sleep or attempted sleep in the motor pool tent, and then Sergeant Hopkins -- he was Private Hopkins then -- and I started back over the ten-odd miles of trail and drifted snow. Hopkins cursed freely in the pre-dawn darkness. I was too cold to object, and when the jeep suddenly skidded to one side, I swore, too.

"And you couldn't get the jeep out of the ditch?"

"No, Sir. We tried, but we couldn't, so Colonel Waverly said we'd wait, a truck would come along." The sergeant was speaking freely under the gentle prodding of the trial counsel. I came back relaxed, trying to focus my wandering mind on the testimony. I wondered what the prosecution was trying to establish other than that I had been captured.

"So you waited?"

"Yes, Sir, for a couple of hours at least. Until just after dawn when we heard rifle fire not far away. Colonel Waverly said he was going to find out what was up. He went down the road, and I followed him."

"Were you armed?"

"Colonel Waverly was, Sir, with a pistol. I left my carbine at the regiment."

"What happened then?"

"Colonel Waverly took off his shoulder insignia and threw them away, and then told me to wait while he went on."

"Did he give any reasons for his actions?"

Of course not, you fool. To a private? I threw my eagles away because I was afraid and I didn't want to get bayoneted. It's common enough. It's the sensible thing to do. I heard the rifle fire grow in intensity, and then machine guns, ours high-pitched and theirs low in the sub-zero air, and I was afraid. Not for myself, but for the regiment and myself. And for Private Hopkins. He was so young, so bewildered. So I went on alone over the crest of the hill and down the other side, dragging my heavy boots and numb feet through the drifts. I had to get through to the regiment. I was a fool for having left it.

I glanced back once. There was nothing behind me but snow, a rolling, enveloping white sea of it marred only by my lumbering path. Hopkins was gone. I never saw him again until now. I went forward into the snow, trying to go faster, listening to the firing and wanting to stop and vomit the heaviness and the fear out of me. But there wasn't the tiine and whatever was in me couldn't be eliminated as easily as that.

The ground somewhere beneath me rolled suddenly upward, and I slipped and fell, sprawling full-length on my face. I lay there, a minute or an hour, whatever it was, and then got to my feet. I went on up the hill toward the firing. The heaviness had spread all over my body. I fell again near the top of the hill.

It was hard to remember; four years that had no beginning and no end, four years that were longer than the forty that had gone before, four years of fear and the attempt to forget and now this. It had happened, it had been part of me, and yet now, in this hot August courtroom, it had never been. Even this was a dream, a warm, uncomfortable, impossible dream. My defense counsel touched my elbow, smiling reassuringly at me. He, too, was part of the dream that I could only escape when I woke and was free of the heaviness and the fear inside me.

The little sergeant looked at me again, rose, saluted the court, and turned away out of my sight. Someone else took his place, someone I didn't know, and there was talk, the intonation of the meaningless military rite of introducing a witness. I looked away, hearing only the sound of words without cadence or meaning and then stared down at my hands, ignoring the eyes that focused on me and the finger that pointed. All I knew was the heaviness as I reached the top of the hill, that was still inside me.

Blindly, I had walked into their arms. I, Colonel John Waverly, Infantry, United States Army, walked blindly into the arms of a squad of quilt-clad members of the so-called People's Volunteers, and the four years began. They shook me, cuffed me, prodded me, and then I went on like a sheep, hearing occasional high-pitched voices as I plodded among them through the snow, listening to the fading gunfire far off and waiting for the sudden sharp pain and then oblivion I had long-ago taught myself to expect. But not like this; good God, not like this, I kept telling myself. It was the only conscious thought I could remember.

My defense counsel touched my elbow; I almost jumped at the sudden sensation but caught myself in time. I was sure no one noticed as I glanced down at the pad he was writing on. He pushed it in front of me, and I read it quickly.

"Do you know anything about this one?" he had written, and nodded toward the witness chair. I looked at the man occupying it--another sergeant, a stocky master sergeant with blunt, weather-browned features and heavy lines etched across his forehead, the type of non-com who is a treasure in an outfit, who takes the detail out of your hands and does what has to be done with it, the type who sees everything in unimaginative black and white. As far as I knew, I'd never seen him before. I looked at Scott again and shook my head.

"Listen to him carefully," Scott scrawled hurriedly on the pad. "This may be important."

I looked back at the man; he, too, sat tensely on the unfamiliar chair, staring straight ahead as he spoke in a nasal mountain monotone. There were so many like him all through the army that he did seem familiar.

"Then, when the Chinks woke us up an I looked around, I saw this guy they'd shoved in durin the night. I could tell he was an officer."

"Do you see him in this room?" The trial counsel spoke in a so carefully-enunciated, soothing voice, and yet behind it I could sense a triumphant self-confidence.

"Yessir, over yonder, Sir." He pointed, and again there were the eyes. I stared at the sergeant; he stared back until the trial counsel spoke

'Can you tell us what took place while the accused was in your presence?"

"Like I said, the Chinks woke us up. It was cold, colder'n. . .cold." Someone in the room tittered; the sergeant flushed and then went on: "They brought in a bucket of cold rice, the gray, dirty-lookin kind. The rest of us ate it. We knew it was all we was goin to get. The colonel, the accused, that is, didn't take any. He just sat over in the corner, not sayin anythin to anybody."

"Can you describe the appearance of the accused?"

"Yessir. He looked pretty dirty like the rest of us."

"Did your captors single him out for any special attention?"

"Nossir. Not then, that is. Later they did."

"That same day?"

"That one or the next one. I don't remember which."

"Can you describe the circumstance, Sergeant?"

"Well, they hadn't bothered us none, cept for feedin us once or twice, an they come in an took the accused out."

"Did he offer any resistance?"

"Nossir. It was kind of like he was asleep, Sir, or like a blind man. You couldn't resist anyway, Sir."

I mentally thanked the sergeant. The straw in the whirlwind is unconscious, unresisting until the exhausted air drops it to earth. It lies there until the next time.

"How long was he gone, Sergeant?"

"A couple of hours, I guess. It was hard to tell."

A couple of hours, Sergeant? Or a couple of years or of lifetimes or eons? An eternity of standing naked and alone while the Chinese captain smiled politely between questions. An eternity of cold helplessness, fearing to look down to see the white skin, struggling to maintain some semblance of the human dignity that you lost when they stripped you. A couple of hours.

The captain's face was youthful, the eternal youthfulness that so many Chinese possess, and his English was precise in spite of its alien tempo.

"And you are with the 425th regiment, Colonel?"

"I gave you my name, rank, and serial number."

"Most assuredly you did. So sorry. I forgot. The road was long and hard from Inchon. And now your regiment is no more. It must be hard to be a colonel, to consign young men to death, and then to attempt to sleep at night, knowing your regiment has been wiped out of existence."

I prayed I didn't show my shock. "The 425th has a hundred years of history behind it. It will go on. Men make no difference."

He smiled politely. "The 425th! Thank you, Colonel." He wrote on a slip of paper.

"You bastard." The words barely came out.

The smile drew into a grin. "Your quarters are quite comfortable, Colonel?"

I said nothing.

"Korean roads and Korean winter present serious supply problems. An officer's life is difficult and unappreciated. Ammunition, especially, is scarce. And your supply line is so long. You must have had difficulty."

I stared at the wall behind him. The stream-worn fieldstone and gray-white mortar swam in strange geometric patterns before my eyes. His voice, highpitched and monotonous, droned on. I shut the words out of my mind. My legs ached; my stomach reeled. In spite of the cold, perspiration ran out of my armpits, drawing icy fingers down my sides. The voice went on and on and on. Only a couple of hours. As far as I know, I said nothing.

"And you were awake when the accused returned, Sergeant?"

"Yessir. It was still daylight."

"How did the accused look when he returned?"

Colonel Scott jumped to his feet. "Objection!"

The law officer smiled. "Will you rephrase the question?"

A note of annoyance crept into the trial counsel's voice. "Will you describe what the accused was wearing?"

"He had on a blue Chinese overcoat."

"Thank you, sergeant." He turned away, smiling at Scott. "Your witness, Colonel."

It was futile, but Scott rose. "Were you ever issued a Chinese overcoat, Sergeant?"

"Nossir."

"No further questions," Scott said. He raised his eyebrows at me quizzically as he sat down. He, too, knew it was futile. How could the sergeant or anyone know that they had returned my clothes, indeed had helped me put them on, and then discovered my field coat was gone? The captain ordered a search, smiled "So sorry," and then produced the blue one. I began to shake, put it on, and went back to the room.

The room, the cold, mud-walled room, the men huddled lifelessly and alone, where your stomach swelled and you emptied your bladder and the swelling came back, and you tried painfully and uselessly to empty it again and the minutes were endless, the days undefined and then you saw that the other huddled men were gone, where or when, you had no idea; and you were alone and you ate something gray and sour and pasty and you vomited and shivered and slept and tried to make water and then stood again, naked and alone, and stared at the fieldstone wall, shutting out the polite smile, listening helplessly to the voice. And then back to the room where time was a lie.

Scott touched my arm again, indicated the pad, and then smiled. "It's all right," he'd written. "A detail. Clear it up on the stand." I nodded as I stared behind him at a fly, buzzing and beating his life away against a window pane, unable to penetrate the impervious glass. It was all right, a detail, a microscopic mote in the eye of eternity.

Someone said once, during the war, that there are no atheists in foxholes, and immediately it was broadcast as truth. Equally true although unacknowledged is the absence of God in a mud-walled room. Perhaps he was busy or had misplaced man for what to him was a moment, and winter became spring and water ran from the walls and still you were alone. They gave you some medicine once and you gagged and slept and learned to eat the foul paste and if you had noticed, you would have seen that it was summer.

And then there were dreams. Awake or asleep, you had dreams, vivid ones that were reality while they lasted; the sudden, clear image of an iron fence in the old part of town; a busy street corner somewhere in space and time; your wife, young and in love, turning to you; the faint, frightened cry of your child. And then you awoke to face the questions, the slop, the walls, the emptiness of being alone. That day in early, steaming summer when they said you had a visitor, you were terrified. Even washed, shaven, fed, clothed in new blue trousers and blouse, you were afraid. Outside was the world; inside the walls and yourself was the only reality, the formlessness of time and dreams.

The fly's buzzing seemed less angry, less determined, as if he was realizing the futility of continuing his assault on the glass. 1 watched him for a moment as he crawled slowly across the clear surface and then I looked back at my counsel. He was staring down at the charge sheet on the table in front of him. A bead of perspiration ran down the side of his face. He wrote something rapidly on a pad, then put it to one side.

I looked up then; somehow, someone else was in the witness chair, the trial counsel was asking questions. After a moment he turned away, took something from his table and then held it up, still smiling confidently. He had a photograph, a shiny enlargement in his hands. Suddenly I thought of the visitor; he had taken a picture. I looked at the man in the witness chair, a civilian, thin, well-dressed, ill-at-ease.

Walking across to the court reporter's desk, the trial counsel held the photograph up. "I request that the reporter mark this exhibit for identification."

The reporter, a small master sergeant wearing huge horn-rimmed glasses, took the photograph and wrote something on the back of it. He handed it back. "This will be Prosecution Exhibit A for identification."

"Thank you." The trial counsel turned and placed the picture on the desk in front of Scott and me. "You may examine it," he said and stepped back.

I recognized myself immediately, seated in front of a low stone building. My face was thin, and I was making an effort to smile; I don't know why, unless it was some wild, illogical hope that my wife, Jean, would see the picture. Or maybe it was in answer to the low urging of the Chinese captain who stood beside the man who took the picture. l remembered trying to decide what the man was. He was white; I could see that for myself, and the Chinese volunteered no information. I don't remember thinking any more about it, but I must have assumed he was one of them. Scott released his hold on the photograph, and the trial counsel took it and turned back to the man in the witness chair.

"Do you recognize Prosecution Exhibit A for identification?"

"I do. It is an enlargement of a photograph which I took on or about June 15, 1951."

"How do you recognize it as the same?"

"I remember the subject and the setting. Both of them are clear and recognizable in the print."

"Can you tell us the circumstances under which you took the photograph, Mr. Grim?"

"I was a civilian photographer assigned as a war correspondent to the Eighth Army in Korea. In December, 1950, I was captured by the Chinese. After about six months' imprisonment, the Reds gave me a camera and film and put me to work taking pictures of the other P.O.W.'s. I assumed it was for propaganda purposes, but I was in no position to argue. As I said, I took the picture in June of 1951 in North Korea."

"Can you tell us of the circumstances surrounding the taking of that particular picture?"

The man leaned forward, cleared his throat, and wiped his mouth on the back of his hand. "That morning I was taken from the place I was imprisoned and given the camera and three film packs. The Chinese captain who was in charge of my guards on those occasions said I was going to take some pictures of a high-ranking officer. 1 asked the captain if he meant General Dean. He said no, that it was a colonel."

"We drove about thirty miles to a small Red camp. In the middle of it was a wire enclosure around a small mud building. The Reds brought a man out. He was wearing blue clothing, the type they issued to P.O.W.'s.

"Do you see the man in this room?"

"Yes, sir. The accused." He looked at me for a moment. I tried to remember his face, but it was no use.

"What else transpired at that time?"

"They seated him in front of the building and I took the picture." The man's voice dropped. He seemed reluctant to say anymore, and he glanced quickly in my direction. I tried to smile to show him that it was all right, that I understood, but he looked away as the trial counsel spoke.

"Did he seem to get on well with his captors?"

Scott jumped up. "I object. The trial counsel is asking the witness to nake an assumption."

The law officer leaned forward and folded his hands on his desk. "Objection sustained. The court and witness will ignore the question, and the trial counsel will phrase his questions in a manner that will not jeopardize the determination of fact."

The trial counsel flushed slightly. "Can you tell us, Mr. Grim, what you observed of the relations between the accused and his captors?"

"Very little, I'm afraid." He paused for a minute and then went on. ' They brought him out, I focused and loaded the camera, took three exposures, and we left."

"Did you speak to the accused?"

"No, sir. I wasn't permitted to."

"Did anyone speak on the occasion?"

"Yes, sir. The captain in charge of the prisoner was trying to get him to smile."

"What did he say?"

"It wasn't so much what he said. He acted like a father trying to get his son to smile at the birdie."

"Would you say he was on familiar terms with the accused?"

"I'd say he was condescending, like parents sometimes are."

The trial counsel paused dramatically and looked slowly down the line of khaki-clad officers who sat on the court. He turned again to the witness.

"Did the accused say anything?"

"No, sir."

"Did he smile?"

"I would say he tried to."

"Did the accused's captors say anything about him to you?"

The man cleared his throat again and glanced at me. Then he looked at his hands folded in his lap. "Yes, one of them did."

"What did he say?"

"He said the accused was his favorite prisoner, well behaved and very cooperative."

"Did he emphasize the last word?"

"It was difficult to tell."

The trial counsel turned away. "The prosecution has no further questions." He placed the photograph on the desk in front of the president of the court. "Prosecution Exhibit A for identification is offered in evidence as Prosecution Exhibit A." The president glanced at it and then looked at me. I watched the retreating back of the trial counsel, hardly hearing the law officer's acception of the picture in evidence. Scott touched my shoulder reassuringly as he rose to question the witness. I turned to look at the window. The fly was still crawling slowly across the pane.

Scott was questioning the man, slowly and carefully, and more often than not, the answers used the word propaganda. It recurred like a theme, and Scott stressed it carefully as he restated the man's testimony. I saw a colonel on the board nod his head in agreement, and I felt momentarily elated. Of course it was propaganda; they were masters of that. What else could it be?

And then I remembered. Just after that the conferences started. It was more than propaganda; it was used as a club. They promised to send it to Jean so that she would know I was well. She would show it to the children, put it on the mantle, look up at it as she prayed, as she wrote the letters I never received. She would know I was well. I even heard the captain's voice in my dreams. She would know I was well.

Of course, I would have to be alert at the conferences. I would have to listen carefully to the captain and the young lieutenant who came along sometimes, and I would have to read the pages they assigned in the books they provided. It was an easy task, the kind that would be assigned a child, and the picture was the gold star on my paper, the mark of approval. There were no questions in my mind; perhaps Scott leaned over toward me. "From here on, it's going to be rough. We've got to be on our toes. For God's sake, don't miss anything." His whisper was low, but he might as well have shouted. Three of the officers on the board looked over at us. One of them frowned. I nodded to Scott as I watched the next witness, another enlisted man, go through the formality of taking the oath and identifying himself. I looked down at the pad on the table as he pointed toward me, but this time I didn't feel the impact of the eyes on me because I suddenly recognized the man in the witness chair, and I had thought he was dead. He deserved to be, and they told me he was. I believed them and now here he was, alive or a ghost, to damn me. As I looked up, he seemed to be studying me. Then he turned back to the trial counsel.

"You were a prisoner of war in Korea, Corporal Slade?"

"Yes, Sir."

"You were acquainted with the accused during that time?"

"Yes, Sir, I was."

"What were the circumstances under which you were acquainted?"

The trial counsel didn't have to ask. He could read any one of the twenty or more depositions I made and signed since Panmunjon. They were all on file someplace, probably lost among thousands of similar papers from the past half-dozen wars. If the trial counsel wanted them, he shouldn't have too much trouble finding them. He had raised a witness from the dead; anything less should be easy. But I remembered that I hadn't mentioned the corporal in any of the depositions. Whether I had forgotten or had been afraid or ashamed to, I didn't know; what mattered was that he was here. Suddenly I realized what it meant. The rest was preliminary, details, as Scott had said. This was the goods, and there was no explanation except the obvious one, the one the court would hear now.

"The accused was senior prisoner officer in the camp. Is that right?"

"Yes, Sir, he was."

"How many prisoners were in the camp?"

"About four hundred, more or less. It varied considerably."

"Did you come into contact with the accused frequently?"

"Yes, Sir."

"How did that happen?"

"I was one of the guys the Chinks call reactionary cause we didn't have anything to do with em, so I caught a good many of the dirty details, sanitary details, especially. And we were responsible to the accused, Sir."

"What were your duties?"

"Mostly latrine work. Digging the pits and keeping them clean and filling them in and so on. Then, too, we worked on grave details and emptying the slop from the shacks we slept in. It was pretty messy work, Sir."

"I can well imagine. And during these duties, how did you come in contact with the accused?"

"He used to assign the jobs and come around to check up on us. He watched us pretty close most of the time."

"Were you punished at any time during the course of this work?"

"Yes, Sir, twice. Some of the guys were more than that."

Scott jumped up. "I object. This line of questioning has nothing to do with the case at hand, and it tends to cast aspersions on the accused without due cause."

The trial counsel held up his hand, palm outward, toward the law officer. "Sir, I expect to show relationship to the case and to the charges and specifications in the case. May I continue?"

The law member sat back and tapped his pencil on the desk for a long moment. It was the only sound in the room unless others could hear my heart. My mouth went dry, and I closed my eyes for a moment.

"Objection overruled. You may continue."

"Thank you." The trial counsel turned again to the witness. The corporal was perspiring heavily; he wiped his brow with the back of his hand. The trial counsel smiled sympathetically. "Who administered these punishments, corporal?"

"The Chink guards, Sir."

"Was the accused present at any time?"

"No, Sir. Not while I was gettin it." He looked directly at me.

The trial counsel paused a moment for effect and looked slowly around the courtroom. As his eyes rested momentarily on me, I felt sick. There was a knot of fear in my stomach, and I could feel the perspiration run down my sides in little cold drops. I wanted to jump up, to shout no, to tell him how wrong he was, but most of all I wanted to run. But I sat there, knowing there was no way to stop it, no way to make them understand, no way I could ever justify anything I did or said during that time; there was nothing I could do except sit there and take it and remember how it was. Maybe then I could put it together and find some logical reason they could accept. But most of all, I needed an explanation that I could accept and live with. I thought I had one then; in the months before the trial I had learned that, too, was a lie I had wanted to believe.

They had moved me north at the end of September; the month was suddenly clear in my mind. They told me I had done well in my studies and as a reward I was being sent north to another camp where I could help my fellow prisoners. They needed recreation and educational facilities; they had to be taught the rudiments of sanitation; they had to be taught to live together for the good of all of them collectively; they emphasized that a great deal of the responsibility for all this would be mine. It was my duty to my subordinates and to my fellow men to look out for them, to teach them to care for themselves.

The Chinese captain spoke convincingly, or else I convinced myself. Anyway, I went north with the idea that I would do my best.

I forced myself to concentrate on the witness's testimony; as Scott said, it was important, much more so than anything that had gone before. There was even more than that involved, too. There were vague, unphrased doubts in my mind. Perhaps for my own sake I could determine whether or not I was guilty. The witness's voice droned on; as he told about the camp, 1 could see it in my mind.

The camp was located in a narrow valley between high, rocky hills, and a rapid little stream ran through the middle of it, just skirting the weatherbeaten board buildings inside the wire. There were guard towers spotted around the perimeter of the wire, and far up on one hillside I saw the glint of the sun shining on a machine gun barrel. As we approached the enclosure, I wanted to run -- back to my mud walled room, back to my dreams. In spite of the heat of the late fall day, I began to shiver. I didn't know what to expect except faces -- unfamiliar American faces -- and voices that spoke in half a dozen different accents, none of them highpitched or sing-song. After nine months of the room, the questions, the dreams, I was terrified. I was afraid to face anything else. I wanted to run.

I forced myself to look at the stream. There were men clustered along its edges, washing, drinking, staring at its turbulent surface. Some of them walked slowly along its bank. It ran close beside a canvas-covered enclosure that could have only one purpose. In spite of the speed of the current, I knew that sanitation would be a problem. The camp was ideally located from a security point of view; it was also ideally located for the spread of disease. The small truck we were riding in stopped at the gate, and my terror disappeared. I would have something to do, something that would bring me back to the world of the present. I was almost exhilarated as the guard motioned me toward the gate.

The witness mentioned my name. I forced my mind back to the present. His eyes were half-closed, and his strained face told that he, too, was reliving the past.

"There was four of us in on the plot. We figured with luck and a good, hard storm, we would make it. We made blackjacks out of scraps of clothes with rocks, in them, and we had a couple of pieces of shovel handle that we'd hid till the time came. We was just waiting for a break."

"How long had you been planning your escape, corporal?"

"Three or four months, I guess. I don't remember."

"Before or after the accused was transferred to your camp?"

"Both, sir, as far as I remember."

"Was the accused told of your plans?"

"We didn't tell anybody, Sir. There were a lot of guys we called *progressives* around, and we wasn't taking any chances."

"What do you mean by *progressives*, corporal?"

"Well, like I said, the Reds gave lectures that they made us attend. Some went and gave no troubles and got along pretty well with the Chinks. The lecturers said that they were progressing, so we called them *progressives*. The rest of us, who wouldn't go along with that, was reactionaries. The Chinks started the names, Sir. We just took them up."

"Thank you. And you say that there were a great many *progressives* in your camp?"

"Not a great many, Sir. Some. But you could never be sure when somebody would figure what the hell and turn. They got a lot better chow than the rest of us, and they wasn't watched so close and didn't catch the dirty details. It was tempting, sir, especially after a year or so."

"These men would trade their loyalty for personal comfort?"

"You could say that, sir."

"And you used the Communist term *progressive* to describe them?"

"Yes, sir."

"Since you were afraid of some unknown *progressive* informing on you, you told no one of your plans to escape."

"No, sir. Nobody. But we was watched mighty close, and you couldn't be sure."

"You say your escape was planned before you knew the accused. Tell us as much as you remember about the circumstances surrounding it."

"One day in the first week of October it rained all day. It was what we was waiting for, good weather to cover us. We figured on going that night when the crick was running good and high. We figured we had a pretty good chance. Like I said, the weather was so bad, we didn't go out on detail that day. We figured on laying around our shack, resting up and sleeping. We'd need all we could get."

There were a good many things the corporal was omitting, and I almost shouted out in court. He was dividing everything into the neat little categories of black and white that the court demanded, and the members were hanging onto his every word. They had all forgotten the innumerable shades of gray in between. Even Scott, sympathetic and believing as he was, looked at me sometimes with an expression of doubt mixed with a shadow of disgust on his face. I could tell them all they were wrong, shout it at the top of my voice, and all of them would turn to me with expressions of doubt and disgust just as Scott did in spite of himself. I dropped my hands in my lap and listened to the corporal's words. There was a great deal of emotion in his words; he glanced over at me, and a brief, satisfied smile crept across his face.

"We fell out for chow as usual and then took our slop back to the shanty to eat. Just after we finished the accused came in. He said he had some work for us."

Of course I had work for you, I almost shouted out. There was always work to be done in spite of the selfishness of the few like you. You're heroes now, you and your friends, because you resisted indoctrination, because you were captured but not defeated. You're white and the rest of us are black. The colors are so clearly defined, aren't they, corporal, aren't they, trial counsel, aren't they, all of you, secure in your stronghold, the Uniform Code of Military Justice?

There was work for you and your friends because I had more than one man could possibly do, and I knew that you and your friends were strong because you saved your strength at the expense of the others--the sick men who became sick because they were hungry, while you and your friends lived well on the food you were stealing for yourselves. Of course I had work for you because you were among the few who were fit to work. And, as always, you wouldn't unless you were driven to it. I was forming the words on my lips as the picture became clearer.

All during the storm I had been going from building to building within the compound. The stream had been rising steadily until it was over its banks, eating at the foundations of the flimsy structures. There were a great many sick, with amoebic dysentery, flu, even a case or two of typhus, and they had to be moved to safer quarters on higher ground. It had to be done fast, and strong backs were needed. I knew where to find them.

The snug, warm little building built and used exclusively by Slade and his friends was on the high ground, well away from the stream, and it was strongly built and dry. It even had a floor, built out of lumber that I knew had come from the wall or roof of one of the other buildings. But that was a minor detail, although I thought as I entered that sooner or later they would have to answer for it. More immediate were the two things I had come for -- their help and their building.

As I entered I saw them sprawled out on makeshift beds, with their heads drawn closely together, playing a corruption of a Japanese children's game with bits of smooth sticks. I stood there in the doorway, letting my eyes get accustomed to the dim interior. Finally one of them looked up.

"Close the door when you leave, Buster." He looked back down and shouted as his partner scored a point.

"All of you men get on your feet. I've got work for you."

One of them rolled over on his back and looked at me. "You got work, you'd better go do it. We ain't budgin out of here. You want us to get sick or something?"

Another one laughed. "Yeah, scram, grandpa. We're all in the same boat here. You want slaves, be your own. The war's over. Sit down and have fun."

"This is a serious matter. We've got to move sick men up on high ground. Get up, all of you."

"Let em drown if they're too sick to move. They're no good, anyway. No sense gettin in a sweat about it."

"I'm giving you men a direct order. Get on your feet and out of here right now, or suffer the consequences."

No one moved. One of the men shouted as he scored a point. I walked over and kicked him in his ribs. He jumped to his feet. "Get out of here, grandpa, before I throw you out. And stay out, or by God, you'll wish you had." He started toward me; the other men shouted and jumped to their feet. One of them brandished a piece of shovel handle. I turned toward the door; somebody stepped in front of me. As I pushed him aside, somebody struck me from the rear.

The corporal's voice rose with excitement, distracting me, forcing me to listen to him. "After we told him we was sick, he kicked me in the ribs and said I'd be a lot sicker if I didn't get up. He said we'd pay plenty if we didn't turn out right away. Then he went out the door. We knew he was going to tell the Chinks, and that we'd better get out of there. We got the stuff we'd hid all together and we headed for where the crick went under the wire."

It happened so soon, then. I had assumed that it was that night, but in fact, until now I wasn't sure that there had actually been an attempt at escape. All I knew was what the guard commander had told me in repressed, high-pitched fury somewhere in the hazy borderland between consciousness and oblivion during the three or four years that followed.

As I reached the door I remembered vaguely that there was another blow, a heavy one that sent me reeling out into the rain, and I struggled through the heavy mud and the swirling overflowed water toward the threatened shacks. They were islands in the roaring brown turbulence. As I neared them, one moved slightly and then went over on its side. I heard men shouting, I knew that I had to get to them, and then everything became black and still.

The corporal's voice filled in the void. "We got through the water to where the stream went through the wire on the upstream end, the way we wanted to go back in the hills, but it was too deep and rapid, so we started to work our way downstream to the other end. We figured maybe the water'd torn the wire so we could get through. When we were about halfway down, we saw a couple of squads of Chinks come at us on the double. We started to run and they opened fire." The corporal's voice dropped. "I was nicked and fell into the stream. When I come to, I was a mile or more away from the camp. I got away."

"And the others, your friends, Corporal?" the trial counsel asked sympathetically.

"I don't know, Sir. I never saw any of them again. They're dead, I reckon, or I would of heard something."

"For your information, Corporal, and for yours, gentlemen," the trial counsel turned to include the court, "The Department of Defense has verified the deaths of those men. I have here an exhibit which I request the reporter mark for identification."

The reporter took the paper and wrote something on it. Then he handed it back. "This will be Prosecution Exhibit B for identification.""

"Thank you." He turned again and then faced our table. He looked directly at me. "I have here Prosecution Exhibit B for identification, a duly authenticated copy of Department of the Army Casualty List Number 427." He placed the paper on the desk in front of us. Scott read it slowly and carefully; I glanced at it, not reading the closely-spaced words. Scott looked up finally and gave it back to the trial counsel. He turned away.

"This is offered in evidence as Prosecution Exhibit B." He handed it to the president of the court; the law officer accepted it in evidence. I felt a heavy knot in my stomach again as the president placed it on top of the photograph.

It's difficult to feel the death of another, no matter how well you may have known him, no matter how that death may affect you. I remembered the pouring rain, but in my excitement and pain and fainting I heard no rifle fire. In fact, I heard nothing for the rest of that day and the next. When finally I awoke, in the little cubicle that was my quarters, my head was bandaged. I lay there trying to remember what had happened. Finally, an American enlisted man came into the room. He came over and looked down at me. Then he saw I was awake.

"Guess you're going to live after all, Colonel."

"What happened?" My head ached, and I could hardly speak.

"Lots of excitement around here, the flood and all, and then the Chinks found you out in the rain and carried you in."

"What else?"

"Nobody knows for sure. We've been restricted to the buildings since, but all kinds of rumors are flying around." He turned away a moment and then looked down at me again. "The guys are saying some pretty nasty things, colonel." I hadn't noticed the coldness in his voice before, but I did then. "Some of the things are about you."

"What kind of things?"

"They're saying some guys tried a break the other night. They're saying you tried to stop it. They're saying there was a lot of shooting, that some guys were killed."

My head throbbed suddenly, and I closed my eyes. He might as well have struck me. The effect was the same. It was impossible to believe, and yet. . . I must have slept or fainted then, because I don't remember any more until the Chinese guard commander came into the room. As nearly as I can figure, it must have been the next day.

"Colonel Waverly!" he said imperiously. I opened my eyes.

"I am glad to see that you are recovering."

I didn't reply.

"You are going to be transferred elsewhere, Colonel. At my request. Immediately you are ready to travel."

"Why, may I ask?" I wasn't sure I had understood him right, and it was effort to speak, but I didn't want to show any anxiety. I vaguely remembered the talk of the shootings, but I wasn't sure whether the enlisted man who had been in my room was real or a dream.

'There is a great deal of unrest among the prisoners. For your own safety and ours, you must be transferred. You are acquainted with the events of the night before last, the night of the flood?" He sounded angry, but under careful restraint.

"I'm not sure. I remember the flood and that's all."

"A group of your countrymen attempted an escape. They were shot, all of them. Some of your men saw you come from their quarters injured. They have connected the two. We know that is not true, but the prisoners refuse to believe us. There has been agitation. You are in danger. You must leave."

Colonel Scott touched my arm, startling me. "You must have something on this guy," he whispered. "We can shake this if I've got something to base my questions on." He glanced at his watch. "It's time for lunch. We'll recess before the cross-examination. That's a break."

The law officer spoke then. "Subject to objection, the court will recess until 1330 hours." He paused a moment and then said "The court is recessed."

We ate a hurried, tasteless lunch of sandwiches at the nearby branch officer's club. As an officer of field grade, I was on my honor. Since I was, according to law, innocent until proven guilty, my honor was still intact, in theory at least, but the stares, the whispers, the indignant snort of one well-fed general officer as we ate, made the whole thing a farce. Suddenly I was glad I had pleaded not guilty. In that moment, as the general stared, I felt angry at the whole affair for the first time. What right had they, all of them, to judge me or anyone else because of a set of circumstances, a photograph, the word of a man none of them would want to accept or keep in his outfit? At first I had hoped to see Jean at lunch in spite of the fact that I told her not to come. Now I was glad she wasn't there.

"Scott, we can discredit his testimony entirely," I said, loudly enough for the general to hear, as I suddenly remembered a clear, shameful incident that was best forgotten. It concerned Slade and another prisoner, an effeminate, emotional soldier who came to me in tears. I told Scott as much of the detail as I could remember.

It was shortly after I arrived at the camp. The place was filthy, especially the barracks and makeshift latrines, and I had the men evacuate some of the buildings and double up in the others while repairs and cleaning were carried out. I assigned a group of men to the shack Slade and his friends had constructed. A day or two later, as I was inspecting the repairs, a young prisoner touched my arm.

"Colonel, I got to talk to you," he said hesitantly.

"Certainly. What is it?"

"I. . .not here, sir. Could we go someplace else?" He looked around quickly; as he looked back at me I saw tears in his eyes.

"What's the trouble, soldier?" I was impatient and I showed it.

"I can't tell you here, sir."

"Come to my quarters at chow time then."

"Yes, sir. I'll be there." He turned away and was gone in the crowd of milling men in fading, formless prisoner's garb.

I had almost forgotten the incident until that night, well after chow, when all the prisoners were supposed to be in their quarters. I was resting, half asleep, thinking of Jean. I was wondering if they'd ever sent the picture. But it wasn't important anymore. I had work to do.

"Colonel," somebody said outside my door.

"What is it?" I was annoyed at being disturbed.

"It's me, Sir. You told me to come," the man said apologetically.

"Come in, man."

He came into my cubicle, holding his hat in his hands. In the twilight he looked to be a young seventeen Then I noticed one of his cheeks was swollen and discolored.

"What's the trouble, son," I said as easily as I could.

"Sir, I. . ." He looked around.

"Sit down first," I said, getting up to make room on the cot. He sat down uneasily; I saw that he was afraid.

"Now tell me what's bothering you."

"Sir, I can't stay in the place you assigned me."

"What's wrong? Having trouble with one of the men? You look as though you were in a fight."

"Not exactly, Sir. I don't know how to tell it."

"One of them bothering you?"

"Yes, Sir. He wants me to do things. He says I'm his girl."

"What?" I jumped to my feet. I'd heard such things, naturally, during my years in the army, but I'd never before actually encountered it. "Are you sure about this?"

"Yes, Sir," he said, and then his voice broke. He was just a confused kid, I could see, and I'd been in the army too long to have many illusions about the men in it. I wasn't doubting him, but he said "Yes, Sir," again. "I wouldn't lie about it."

"It's Slade, Sir," he said. "You know, the big one. He keeps offering me food that he steals."

"You wait here," I said. "I'll take care of Slade." I was angry, and in spite of the fact that it was against regulations, I went over to his shack. I was still angry when I reached his quarters. I went in the door.

"Slade," I shouted. "Which one of you is Slade?"

"Yes, general," one of the men on the floor said lazily. Some of the others laughed.

"Slade, I've just been talking with a man. If I ever talk to another one about the same thing, I'll stop it if I have to kill you with my own hands. I won't stand for perversion. And don't think this is going to be forgotten." I turned to the door. The young soldier had evidently followed me over. "Come along, son," I said. "He won't bother you anymore. If he does, I'll take care of him."

As we left, Slade shouted something about fixing me for being a Chink-loving Red. I ignored it. The young soldier turned to me as we walked back toward my quarters.

"Sir, I shouldn't've told you. That Slade is mean."

"Don't worry about it, son. His kind don't have the guts to do anything but talk."

In spite of my threat, I had forgotten about it until now. Scott listened eagerly until I finished, and then jumped up. "Can you remember the kid's name?"

"I don't think I ever knew it."

"We'll find him somehow. What else do you know about Slade?"

I told him everything I could, and finally he rose. I followed him out.

Scott was a man with long duty in the Judge Advocate's Department and, hence, had innumerable contacts. He spent the rest of the recess on the telephone while I waited, hoping that the boy was still alive, and yet afraid that he wasn't. My hopes were so earnest and desperate that they may have been prayers. Finally Scott came out of the booth. He looked serious.

"We'll get a roster of the men in that camp and work from there. I don't know, though. It won't be easy."

I didn't know either, I thought as we filed back into the courtroom. It was a chance, but a slim one; and now, for the first time, I wanted to win. I had to, for my own sake, for Jean's, for the army, for that piece of paper that they gave me in 1930 to signify trust. The parts were falling into a pattern, but I still didn't know.

The room was hotter, more stifling, than it had been that morning, and the smell of disuse that characterizes court martial buildings was, if anything, stronger. At least it seemed so to me as I watched the formality of reconvening the court. As Corporal Slade took his place in the witness chair and was reminded that he was still under oath, Colonel Scott glanced quickly over the notes he had made for his cross examination. Then he rose and walked slowly over to the stand. Slade watched him with what I hoped was distrust or fear. The man looked at me for a moment and I saw that it was neither. A self-assured smile touched the corners of his lips.

"Corporal Slade," Scott said slowly and then paused until Slade looked up at him. In the silence, the president of the court cleared his throat audibly, and then Scott continued.

"Corporal Slade, you have described the escape in which you participated. Would you say that you were the leader of that attempt?"

"Yes, Sir, 1 guess I was."

"It was unsuccessful only because you were discovered in the act?"

"Yes, Sir."

"How many of you participated?"

"Four."

"And three were killed in the attempt?"

"Yes, Sir."

"And what happened to you? That is, were you recaptured or did you succeed in gaining your freedom?"

"The Chinks caught me a couple of days later. They took me to another camp then and really gave me the works."

"An escape, either attempted or successful, demands a great deal of physical stamina, does it not, corporal?"

"Yes, Sir, it does."

"You were in good enough physical condition to think that your chances of success were good?"

"Yes, Sir."

"And your friends?"

"Yes, Sir. We took good care of ourselves, the best we could."

"The prison ration per man was sufficient to maintain your strong physical condition?"

The trial counsel sprang to his feet. "I object to this entire line of questioning. The witness is not on trial."

The law officer looked at Scott. Scott sighed heavily.

"I propose to show that the witness was prejudiced against the accused due to occasions in the camp during which the accused was forced by the actions of the witness to intercede to protect the right of the rest of the prisoners."

"Objection overruled," the law officer said then. The trial counsel sat down, but he was smiling. Scott frowned. The witness sat back in his chair. The objection was overruled, but the witness was alert now. He put his elbows on the arms of his chair, folded his hands, and looked up at Scott. The damage was done. There was a long silence. "The witness will answer the question," the law officer directed.

Slade glanced at the trial counsel, who shrugged his shoulders perceptibly, and then looked up at Scott. "Maybe for some it wasn't, sir, but we managed."

"Four of you?"

"Yes, Sir."

"Out of four hundred in the camp?"

"Maybe there was more who were strong enough. I can't say. Like I said, we didn't tell anybody what we planned."

"You were strong enough to escape even though you had to brave a roaring stream and yet you sustained your strength on the same daily rations as the other prisoners?"

Slade hesitated. "We might have got a little extra."

"You might have?"

Slade didn't answer, and Scott didn't wait. "Was the 'extra' given to you by your Chinese guards?"

"No, Sir. We wasn't progressives."

"Then we may assume that the extra food was gained through your own efforts within the camp."

"I object to this speculation on the part of defense counsel," the trial counsel shouted from his seat. "The witness is not on trial, as I said before," he continued more calmly as he got to his feet.

"I assume that defense counsel is pursuing this line of questioning for the reason stated before," the law officer said.

"Yes, Sir," Scott said quietly.

"You may continue."

Scott turned to Slade quickly. "Corporal, were you ever punished because you stole food from the prisoners' mess?"

"I object," the law officer shouted again.

"The admission of punishment is not admission of guilt on the part of the witness. Objection overruled. The witness will answer the question," the law officer stated.

"Yes, Sir, I was," Slade answered hesitantly. "But it was only from the progressives," he said hurriedly.

"Were these the punishments at which the accused was present?"

"I. . .don't remember, Sir."

"There were others?"

"Yes, Sir. A lot of them."

"Why, may I ask?"

"Because we caught the dirty details, that's why."

"Latrine detail?"

"Yes, Sir. That's what you could call it."

"And helping with the sick?"

"Yes, Sir."

"And cleaning details?"

"Yes, Sir."

"The accused was in charge of assigning these details?"

"Yes, Sir."

"And you were strong? Strong enough to carry them out?"

"Yes, Sir, I guess I was."

"Could you by any stretch of the imagination construe any of those acts as aiding, abetting, or giving comfort to the enemy? Were not those duties among those which any soldier may be lawfully ordered to perform?" Scott almost thundered the question.

"I . . . I guess so, Sir." Slade's voice was almost inaudible. He was clasping and unclasping his hands repeatedly. For a moment I almost felt sorry for the man. Then I remembered the young soldier and his fear, and Slade's insolence and the feeling was gone. I felt like applauding Scott for doing what I would never be able to do. Scott was merciless, and Slade seemed to shrink in his seat.

Scott turned away a moment as if to gather his thoughts, and then turned quickly to face Slade.

"On the day of the attempted escape, you encountered the accused, did you not?"

"Yes, Sir."

"In your quarters?"

"Yes, Sir."

"It was raining heavily?"

"Yes, Sir."

"Can you describe the condition of the camp as a result of that rain?"

"Well, like I said, the stream that ran through it was flooded, higher than I ever saw if before. Some of the camp was under water."

"Were any of the buildings in the camp located so that they were in danger from the flooded stream?"

" I guess so, Sir."

"And the accused came to your quarters and said he needed your help?"

"He said he had work for us, Sir."

"Removing sick and injured men from the endangered buildings?"

"I don't remember. I don't think he said."

"And you refused his direct order."

"We was planning our escape. He had it in for us. He was buddy-buddy with the Chinks. He was going to turn us in. We couldn't take any chances."

"In that encounter was the accused struck in any way?"

"I. . .I don't remember, Sir."

"With a club?"

"I didn't, Sir. I didn't do it." Slade's face was flushed and he was sweating freely.

"And immediately after this incident, you attempted to escape?"

"Yes, Sir. Right afterwards. He was going to tell the Chinks."

"Wouldn't it have been wiser to forget about the escape for the time being? Wouldn't that have disproved anything he might have told your captors?"

"I object," the trial counsel shouted again. "The wisdom or lack of it is not relative questioning. The facts have been established that these men were forced to attempt an escape through fear of the accused and his relationship with the enemy. The defense counsel should confine his questioning to the facts of the case."

Scott turned slowly to face the law officer. "Sir, the present questioning is designed to show that the accused had no knowledge of any impending escape, that even if he had, he was in no position to communicate such knowledge to the enemy. He was unconscious due to a blow on the head. If this escape was attempted, it was through fear that retribution would be exacted by the accused upon return to United States military control. Fear of retribution by the Chinese was not the motive; the attempt to discredit the accused was. This trial is evidence of that."

The law officer nodded. "Defense counsel's reasoning is in order; however, in the future he will confine his questions to establishment of the facts. The witness need not answer the question. It calls for opinion on the part of the witness."

Scott nodded slowly and then turned away. "Corporal Slade, from your previous testimony you indicated that the accused had threatened you with reprisals of one sort or another. Do you recall the circumstances surrounding any of those threats?"

"You mean what caused him to make 'em?"

"I do."

"It's pretty hard to remember, Sir. It was mostly about our work. He was always pickin on us, trying to get us to do whatever the Chinks wanted."

"Did the accused ever threaten to kill you, Slade? Kill you with his bare hands?"

"Yes, sir, he did." Slade answered eagerly, sitting forward in his chair. Beads of sweat glistened on his brow.

"Do you remember exactly what caused that threat?"

"Off hand, no, Sir, I don't. I remember him making it, though."

"You're quite sure that he did?"

"Yes, Sir."

"Were any of your friends present at the time?"

"Yes, Sir."

"Where did it take place?"

"In my quarters, near as I can remember."

"Was it daylight or dark?"

"Just about dark, sir. After evening chow."

"You remember all these circumstances and yet you do not remember what caused the accused to make that threat."

"That's right, Sir." Slade wiped the sweat off his face with a handkerchief and then stared at it as he folded it. When he looked up at Scott, his eyes shone like a puppy's, wanting affection and expecting a kick.

Scott stared at him, but waited until Slade put the handkerchief back in his pocket. Then, in a calm, deceptive voice, he went on."Corporal Slade, when the accused threatened your life, did the incident involve another prisoner?"

"I . . . Don't remember, Sir."

"Did the accused tell you that if you ever made abnormal advances toward a fellow prisoner again, he would kill you with his bare hands? Was that why, Slade?" Scott almost shouted the question.

"I object," the trial counsel shouted out as he got to his feet. "Defense counsel is consistently ignoring the case at hand. This questioning has no bearing whatsoever on the guilt or innocence of the accused."

Scott turned to the law officer. "Sir, it doesn't matter. I have no further questions at this time."

The law officer looked relieved as he turned to the trial counsel. "Do you have any further questions, counsel?"

"No, Sir. Not at this time."

"Does any member of the court have any questions?"

After a long silence, the president of the court leaned forward and folded his hands on the table top as he looked at the witness. "Corporal Slade, at the time of your escape, the camp was partially flooded?"

"Yes, Sir."

"Men's lives were in danger from that flood?"

"I guess so, Sir."

"Did accused order you to assist in removing them to safety?"

"He said he had work for us, Sir. That's all."

"On that occasion was accused struck with a weapon of some sort?"

"I'm . . . I'm not sure." Slade mopped his face again. "I didn't do it, I swear." He folded his handkerchief as the president of the court sat back in his chair and turned to the law officer. "That's all I have," he said, and wrote something on the pad of paper in front of him.

The law member then looked slowly down the line of officers on the board. "Any other questions?"

Heads shook slowly. "No," someone said.

"The witness is excused."

"Subject to recall," Scott said as Slade started to get up.

"Subject to recall," the law member repeated. He instructed Slade not to discuss his testimony outside the court room.

Slade nodded eagerly as he rose, saluted the president of the court, and then executed a faltering about face. I tried to catch his eye, but he looked straight ahead as he marched to the door.

Scott was smiling faintly as he came over to sit down beside me. "That went fairly well," he whispered. "At least they've got something to think about." He sat down, still half-smiling. "They've still got plenty they haven't fired off yet."

"I don't know what," I whispered back, but even as I said it, I felt a gnawing ache of fear as my mind went on probing the months that followed, after Slade had been forgotten. I had been transferred, as the camp commandant said I would be, farther north, almost within sight of the Yalu and Manchuria, although I didn't know it at the time, didn't know it, in fact, for months, until my head wound--X-rays after I was released established it as a fracture--was healed. They had put me in a prison hospital ward, in a cubicle of my own, and there I lay for months, again cut off almost completely from any Americans. I had visitors frequently, too frequently, but they were all Chinese. And they all talked about the same things in the same irregularly cadenced voices.

Scott touched my arm as the trial counsel swore in the next witness, another civilian, a lean, intelligent-appearing man wearing horn-rimmed glasses. "Does this one ring any bells?"

I shook my head. I was certain I had never seen him before. He gave his name; it wasn't familiar at all. When the trial counsel omitted the customary question concerning whether or not he knew me, I knew I was right.

"Did you or did you not serve in the armed forces during the recent Korean conflict?"

"I did, Sir."

"In what capacity?"

"I was a Radioman Second Class, United States Naval Reserve."

"On active duty overseas during that time?"

"Yes, Sir."

"In what capacity?"

"I was a radioman standing monitor watches in the Naval Radio Station in Osaka, Japan, Sir."

"You monitored enemy broadcasts?"

"Yes, Sir. That was my primary duty. I recorded them."

"Thank you." The trial counsel crossed rapidly to his table and picked up what looked like a common phonograph record. He held it up. "I request that the reporter mark this exhibit for identification." He handed it to the reporter.

In a moment the reporter handed it back. "This will be Prosecution Exhibit C for identification."

"Thank you." The trial counsel handed it to Scott. I glanced at it, the fear growing within me. There was a Navy seal affixed to the center of it, a code number, initials, and a date -- April 7, 1952. I was in the prison hospital then, I remembered, almost recovered physically; mentally, however, I could not say. There was so much that had happened in the repetitious visits of the Chinese; there were so many dreams of wild water, of screaming men being shot down, of sick men growing sicker and dying while I stood aside idly; there were dreams in which Jean grew fainter and farther away; there were dreams of a cleaner, greener somewhere far over the horizon, and my visitors explored the dreams and encouraged and stimulated them. I was alone, I was forsaken, I was forgotten by all but my captors, the only ones who were concerned with my existence. They pounded that theme into my throbbing head, and each throb was an eternity, each dream a bit of their words come to life.

But the horror of it all was that I had nothing to do during my waking hours except listen to my visitors and then, after they went, berate myself for my stupidity in allowing myself, a human being, to become a fool and a tool of such unfeeling monsters as the men I had tried to help, as the army, even as my wife appeared in my dreams, far off, tempting, tantalizing, laughing and then vanishing as I reached out to her in my need.

Scott touched my arm again, abruptly forcing me back into the present. "Do you remember anything about this?" he whispered.

"No," I said. "It's possible. God knows, anything is. But I don't remember." I spoke more to myself than to Scott, and it was louder than I realized. Faces turned in my direction, but I ignored them. I was trying to remember. There was nothing but fear, self-doubt, self-hate, and the torture of insinuating voices, crescendoing dreams.

The witness had the record in his hands. He was examining it carefully. He handed it back to the trial counsel. "I do recognize this record. It's one which I made of a Chinese English-language broadcast on April 7, 1952."

"How do you recognize it as being the same?"

"The identifying label is in my handwriting, and so is the date. Those initials in the lower left-hand corner are mine."

The trial counsel turned to face the court. "Prosecution Exhibit C for identification is offered in evidence as Prosecution Exhibit C," he said as he took it from the witness.

Scott jumped to his feet. "I object to the introduction of this record as evidence. A record made of what is alleged to be the accused's voice without his knowledge or permission is not acceptable evidence."

The trial counsel turned to the law officer. "A duly-authenticated official armed services recording of an enemy propaganda broadcast is legitimate and acceptable as evidence in establishing that the accused made such a broadcast. And, as a matter of record, no such allegation has been made. Defense counsel is jumping to conclusions not based on the record."

Scott bit his lip and flushed slightly, but he stood there, waiting for the law officer's decision. The trial counsel's thin lips were raised in a smile. Finally, after what seemed like an hour, the law officer spoke.

"The exhibit, if it contains what is alleged to be the voice of the accused, is not admissible. The witness may testify as to what he observed or heard on any occasion. However, submission of a recording is tantamount to forcing the accused to testify against himself."

The trial counsel smiled self-deprecatorily. "Prosecution withdraws the exhibit." He walked slowly over to his table and magnanimously put the record down. Then he turned again to the witness, still smiling with that air of smug, self-assurance, the same self-assurance and certainty that my visitors had displayed when I could do nothing but listen and dream and hate. I felt a strong, sudden urge to jump up and smash that grin with my fist. Scott sat down then and put his hand on my shoulder for a moment. The simple gesture made me feel better. The trial counsel was merely doing his duty, just as was Scott, just as I had done what I thought was mine.

The trial counsel smiled down at the witness. "On April 7, 1952, you were a naval radio monitor?"

"Yes, Sir. I was."

"You recorded enemy broadcasts on that day?"

"Yes, Sir, it was my regular duty."

"Did any of the broadcasts you recorded that day concern the accused?"

"Yes, Sir, one of them did. It was an evening broadcast."

"Will you tell the court just what you heard during that broadcast?" The emphasis on the work 'heard' was heavy; the trial counsel glanced over at Scott.

"I was standing my regular watch, recording whatever propaganda broadcasts came over our regular communications channels. The records were used for later study and analysis, so I was always pretty careful. I listened as attentively as I could. It was pretty difficult sometimes because most of them fell into pretty definite and crude patterns. But this one was a little different. The Chinese announcer said that a high-ranking American officer was going to speak from North Korea. So I turned up the amplifier and listened."

"Did the announcer identify the officer?"

"Yes, Sir, he did."

"What name did he give?"

"It was Colonel John Waverly, United States Army, he said."

Scott objected immediately, and was as quickly overruled. I wanted to jump up, too, to shout that it was a lie, that it was impossible. But I listened passively with a sort of weird fascination as the witness went on. He might have been participating in the scientific dismemberment of a long-dead skeleton with his sharp, clear, decisive voice as a scalpel. As he went on, I might have been a snake and he the charmer. My fascination I knew to be deadly fear because I couldn't be sure. And the more I realized now that I had to win, the stronger the fear grew within me. Again, part of me wanted to run; the rest of me sat still, listening intently, wanting to know.

"Did the voice of the man alleged to be the accused have any distinguishing qualities?"

"That's difficult to say, sir. It was definitely American, but I don't remember any peculiarities to distinguish it from any other American voice except that there was very little inflection--more of a monotone than anything else, I'd say."

"Can you tell us, as nearly as you remember, just what was said in that broadcast?"

"Yes, sir. The person speaking -- the American, that is -- identified himself as the accused, and he said he was speaking from a prison camp hospital in North Korea someplace. He described the place a little bit, said the place was clean and comfortable and that he was getting excellent medical care. The only trouble was, he said, that occasionally, American fighter-bombers would strafe the place and that a number of men had been killed or wounded."

"Did he use the word 'deliberate' at that time?"

"I don't remember, Sir, whether he did or not."

"Can you remember any voice characteristics when he said it?"

"Objection!" Scott said suddenly as he rose. "The witness testified that the voice was a monotone. Also, the question calls for an assumption on the part of the witness."

"Objection sustained," the law officer said, cutting off a word the trial counsel started to say.

The trial counsel grimaced slightly and then turned again to the witness. "Will you continue telling us that you heard on the broadcast?"

"Yes, sir. Well, it seemed as though all this information about the camp was background, well put-together and sort of impersonal and unreal-sounding somehow, like an amateur reading from a script or something. I've heard a lot of them, and they all sound alike. In the beginning it was a pretty conventional propaganda broadcast, and I turned the amplifier down a bit. Then there was a long pause in the broadcast, and I was afraid I'd turned the amplifier off. I checked and it was all right." The witness paused and rubbed his eyes with his thumb and forefinger for a moment, pushing his glasses up on his brow. Then he sat back in his chair and went on.

"His voice didn't change any when he spoke again, but somehow the words sounded more natural, like he was speaking directly to me or to anyone else who was listening. It was either natural off-the-cuff speaking or else the script writer was a great deal more skillful than those who wrote any of the other Chinese broadcasts I've heard. He spoke directly to his wife, and he called her by name, Jean, I think it was, but he might have been talking directly to those of us who were sitting on our fannies back in Japan or the States."

"Did the voice use that precise phrase?"

"No, sir, it didn't. As I remember, he said something like 'sitting back without feeling for those who are suffering and dying, not caring because you are alive.' It means the same thing, doesn't it? I felt a little mad and, well, a little guilty, sir. It was like a voice from the grave."

"I can well imagine. It had a carefully-calculated effect."

I could well imagine, too, but I couldn't remember. There were so many times like that -- times of bitter denunciation of everyone and everything, somewhere in the world between life and the dream. It was all part of what I had tried to drive deep within me in the year since my release, and now I had to remember what had happened and when and how, and I was afraid that I couldn't.

Scott was listening intently, taking notes in a rapid scrawl. He glanced inquiringly at me. I shook my head, and looked back at the witness with the sudden wild hope that he would give me the key to remembering.

Someone among the newsmen or others sitting in the rear of the room coughed loudly. I lost a few of the witness's words and leaned forward, impatiently ignoring something that Scott whispered in my ear. I had to listen, I had to remember. Nothing else mattered; win or lose, I had to find out about myself. The witness went on in a precise, carefully-modulated voice; it was easy, pleasant, unreal to listen to him. He might have been selling soap to women in pin-curlers.

"He talked less than five minutes -- I timed the record later, on the playback -- but it seemed to be much longer. It was a continuous series of questions or statements phrased like questions; it was difficult to tell which, due to the peculiar monotone of his voice."

"Can you recall any of the questions -- or statements?"

"I mentioned the first one -- the one that had the most impact as far as I was concerned. I'd seen a good many people ship out to Korea, and, well, it made me feel pretty useless -- like a parasite or goldbrick or something."

"You had an extremely important job in Japan, did you not?"

"Yes, Sir, fairly important."

"And the broadcast made you dissatisfied?"

"I suppose so, Sir."

"Then it was an effective propaganda broadcast, at least as far as you were concerned?"

Scott objected immediately and after a moment of technical wrangling, his objection was sustained. The questions were irrelevant and inadmissible, but I wished Scott had not spoken. I needed the answers far more than the trial counsel, the court, or that mythical monster, the United States, before whom I was being tried. The trial counsel smiled with his exaggerated good grace and changed his questioning tactics.

"Can you remember any of the other accusations made in the broadcast?"

"I hesitate to call them accusations, sir, but perhaps that's what they were. Like a conscience, sir."

"Will you answer the question, please?"

"Yes, sir. I do remember some of the other statements he made."

"What were they?" Scott chuckled almost inaudibly, and the trial counsel glared at him as the witness answered.

"One of the things was what right had we to be so self-righteous to think that our cellophane-packaged brand of free enterprise would save the world when a few shiploads of wheat in the right place would do more good both now and in the future."

I remembered that. Suddenly and clearly I remembered it. Somewhere in my dreams I had been back on a hillside in Italy just after World War II, reconnoitering for a suitable bivouac. It was noon; we sat down for chow, opening our cold K Rations. The kids appeared then, from nowhere, with their hungry eyes and pathetic tin pails. Not democracy, not even calorie-counted K Rations could fill those pails and those empty stomachs; not Santa Claus and Uncle Sam, but bread. I think it was the first time I actually hated myself for being a human being. During the war it had been relatively easy to rationalize things like that away, but the war had been over for months, and still the kids were hungry. The Reds had found that dream, though, and explored it thoroughly.

"And was there anything else that you remember?" the trial counsel was asking.

The witness answered something. I didn't hear his words because there was a great deal more I was remembering. It came at me in a rush, a tangled montage of scenes and places and people that had accused me, awake and asleep, during those long months in the prison ward. The Chinese interrogators planted fertile seeds skillfully, and those seeds grew quickly; like trees in rich crevasses in the rocks, they almost shattered my mind. There was the American kid, five months out of high school, who raised his rifle and fired at a rustling bush, then shouted "I got me a gook!" Later, when we went to look, the old woman's sightless eyes stared up accusingly. There was the twelve-year-old girl who went from tent to tent in the bivouac -- a can of C Rations, a candy bar, a few soiled yen -- she cried when I caught her, her eyes pleaded. I turned her loose. What could I do? There was the troop information officer who categorized and itemized relations with the natives, remembering everything except that they were human; there was the general, staunch defender of Midwestern Christianity, whose Japanese mistress came unofficially to Korea.

There were so many things that flew at me in those months, like bats out of a cave, and they all came to rest on my chest as I lay there. Of course, I made the broadcast, and it was, as the witness said, like a conscience, my own conscience, the conscience of my country. It was, as the personable, almond-faced young major told me, the least I could do. I hated myself afterward; in the months that followed I drove it deep in my mind, refusing to acknowledge that I had done it. Now I saw it for what it was, a military and moral offense; I had let them make me a tool, for that I should be justly condemned, for that I was sorry. But the words I would say again, no matter how offensive any listener might find them. I was a tool, yes, and therefore a fool, but the words told what I had forced myself to ignore in the past.

Scott leaned toward me, whispering. "The only thing we can establish is the lack of identity of the voice. This kid is smart, and he's honest. It shouldn't be hard."

No, it shouldn't be hard, I told myself as I nodded to Scott's words. That had been in another world, another self, not the immaculately-clad colonel who sat here now, but a scarecrow who caught a glimpse of the hell of the world's poor; not one who spoke with the authority of silver eagles on his shoulder, but one who whispered because he knew the horror of marching feet in his dreams. It shouldn't be hard, but would it not be better to shout the truth that I was guilty of letting them use me? And that I would say it again?

The trial counsel had finished his questioning; Scott crossed the room to cross-examine. As he caught my eye, he smiled almost imperceptibly. I wondered idly whether it was in reassurance or in self-confidence.

"You were a Navy radioman?"

"Yes, Sir."

"How long?"

"Three years, Sir."

"Are you employed in radio now?"

"T.V., Sir."

"In what capacity?" Scott's questions seemed bitten off.

"A sound recorder right now, sir, but I'm primarily interested in producing and directing."

"Any good at it?" Scott grinned down at him suddenly.

"I think so, Sir."

"Good." Scott's grin faded slowly as though he had just realized the seriousness of the business at hand.

"You've heard a great many voices over radio?"

"Objection!" the trial counsel shouted. "Defense counsel is leading the witness through questioning."

"Will you rephrase the question, please?" the law officer asked.

"Have you heard the human voice broadcast?" Scott asked after a moment.

"Yes, Sir."

"Many times?"

"Yes, Sir."

"Have you ever heard voices over radio and later heard the voices in your presence?"

"Yes, Sir, I have."

"Have you had difficulty in recognizing those voices?"

"No, Sir, not as a rule."

Suddenly I realized what was coming. It shouldn't be difficult, Scott said. I braced myself, waiting for his command to speak. Something clutched at me deep inside; I knew I couldn't trust my voice.

"I am going to ask the accused to speak. Will you listen closely, please?"

The trial counsel jumped to his feet. "I object. This is highly irregular, Sir. It calls for an opinion on the part of the witness."

One of the officers on the board muttered something audibly. I mentally thanked God for the directness of the Army mind. It wouldn't be hard, just as Scott said, if only they let me speak. And I knew that the army, with its demand for black and white, would have me speak.

The trial counsel looked down the line of officers. I saw several of them, including one with a brick-red face, nod their heads. "Objection overruled," the law officer said.

Scott glanced at a note in his hand and then looked at me. "Colonel Waverly," he said, "Will you say 'sitting back without feeling for those who are suffering and dying, not caring because you are alive?' "

I stood then, conscious of all the eyes in the courtroom and repeated the words slowly and distinctly. In the hollowness of the room they sounded theatrical and false, like the type of rhetoric I would tune out on the radio. I sat down slowly then in silence.

'Do you recognize that voice?"

"I. . .can't be sure, Sir. Let me think." He bowed his head.

After a moment, Scott asked, "Would you like it repeated?"

"No, Sir." He looked up then. "This man's vowels are broader."

"Anything else?"

"He speaks much more distinctly."

Scott waited patiently, his hands clasped behind him. Suddenly I was very thirsty. I leaned forward.

"The intonation is different."

Scott smiled encouragingly at him.

"I don't think it's the same voice, sir."

A muted hum rose in the courtroom as the trial counsel jumped up. "I object! This is an opinion on the part of the witness. It is not fact, not evidence!" He crossed to face Scott, his hands on his hips.

"Sir, I established that the witness, trained and experienced in radio voice transmission, was capable of distinguishing between voices and of recognizing voices. I submit that it is direct evidence, sir," Scott said in a heavy voice.

"But the witness isn't sure! He doesn't *think* it's the same."

The law officer turned to the witness. "Can you be more definite in your answer?"

"No, sir, I can't."

The law officer sat back. "Objection overruled. The court will take the answer into consideration and weigh it for what it is worth."

I sat back heavily as Scott said he had no more questions. I realized that I was tired, more tired than I had been in months. I scarcely heard the trial counsel requestioned the witness, reiterating the point that he could not be sure that it was not me. Scott sat down. "At best it's a draw," he whispered. I wondered for whom it was best. I knew I had let them use me, and that was what mattered. I was guilty of that.

The witness was dismissed. I rested my head lightly in my hands for a moment. My palms felt cool and moist on my forehead. I could see a Chinese standing over me, talking earnestly, his mouth moving slowly and persuasively. I couldn't hear any words. Then, as Scott touched me on the shoulder, I heard a voice I thought belonged to the Chinese. "The prosecution rests." I looked up immediately, unable to believe it. As I did so, the law officer glanced at his watch. "The court will adjourn until 0900 hours tomorrow."

Scott and I waited patiently until the others, especially the newspaper men, had left the courtroom, and then we walked slowly out into the full intensity of the mid-afternoon sun. A group of reporters loitered along the gravel path. I thought Scott would avoid them as he had before, but this time he didn't. He led me toward them. A flash bulb, prohibited in the courtroom, popped. Scott smiled as the men gathered around us, throwing out hurried questions:

"Gonna be a little more cooperative this time, Colonel?"

"How does it look from the defense corner?"

Scott held up his hand slightly. "Gentlemen, you may say that Colonel Waverly and I have every confidence that this misunderstanding will be cleared up in the near future."

"That's what you call it, huh?"

"That's what I call it," Scott answered. "After the court martial is over, we'll have a more complete statement for you."

"Come on, Colonel, give us a break. What you going to spring?"

"We're not going to spring anything. The facts will speak for themselves. That's really all I can say, gentlemen." He led me away in the wake of more questions. Another flash bulb popped as we got into Scott's car. Then Scott turned to me. "I've got to clear up a few things at the office. Care to wait or shall I drop you off at the B.O.Q.? We can eat at the club and hash things over a bit later then."

"Drop me at the B.O.Q. I've got a few things to do, too."

"All right."

We drove slowly along in silence for the short half-dozen blocks to my quarters -- the quarters to which I was restricted on my honor as a gentleman and a commissioned officer. Justified or not, the privileges of rank were real, I reflected as we passed two men in faded fatigue uniforms with white P's emblazoned on them. An M.P. with a shotgun walked well to their rear. Simple AWOLs, undoubtedly, the most common offense in the army, either awaiting trial or serving their time, while I, accused of a crime that made theirs look microscopic in comparison, rode past them on my way to my own comfortable quarters and later, a steak at the club.

Scott noticed me watching them; he looked at me amusedly. "Feeling kinship with the masses?"

"Something like that," I answered as we stopped in front of my quarters. I got out slowly.

"Half an hour?" Scott asked.

"Fine." I walked slowly up the path to the door, wondering whether or not I should call Jean. I wanted to badly enough, not to talk or to tell her about the day or to lean on her emotionally as I so often had in the past, but simply to reassure myself that she was still there. If I had been able to do that in the camps, if I could have believed it, although God knows I had no reason to doubt it, except for those vicious seeds planted in me by the Chinese, things would have been different. Or would they? I asked myself as I passed the telephone booths without looking at them. At any rate, it was a possibility, and, if true, a horrifying indictment of my emotional completeness as a man. I ran up the stairs to my room. I couldn't call until I knew whether or not I could go to her with clean hands and a cleansed mind. Technical guilt or innocence didn't matter, but that did, and I knew she would be waiting for my call just as she said she would. And I was afraid that I knew that I had no right to go to her. I was guilty. The broadcast proved that beyond doubt.

I threw myself on my cot in a futile effort to relax for a moment. The sounds of occupancy, of normal, human activity, came through the thin walls -- water running, doors slamming, a telephone ringing -- the things that one didn't think about or let himself think about in the camps. After a moment I got up, walked the narrow floor, staring occasionally out the window at the building opposite, pausing to look down at Jean's picture on my tiny table, and all the time feeling the pressure of the dark brown walls around me. Finally I had to get out of the room. I sat outside on the steps, smoking cigarettes, acknowledging the respectfully distant greetings of the other officers coming and going, until finally Scott drove up. I forced myself to walk slowly out to the car.

After I got in, Scott turned to me. "I talked to Washington about the kid, and I'm afraid we're going to run into trouble locating him unless we can find out who he is. I'll have to ask for an adjournment, for a couple of days at least."

"An adjournment?" I hadn't thought of the possibility.

"Until we can inquire more thoroughly. They'll grant it, without a doubt," he said as he put the car in gear.

"Scott, I'd rather not," I said after a moment. "Do you think he'll make any difference?"

"Probably not. But you never can tell."

"Let's drop it then, and get it over with."

"All right, if you prefer. But there's no point in making things easy for them."

"I'd rather not put things off any longer."

"Whatever you say. But our defense is going to be pretty conventional without him."

Later, as we ate, Scott outlined his plan of defense. As he said, it was pretty conventional; character witnesses who knew me or knew of me in the camps -- a few men who knew what I had tried to do, a number of officers who knew me in the last of the camps just before my release, the chaplain who invited me to that Christmas Mass an eternity ago; medical officers who had probed and X-rayed and treated my head, a soldier who saw the Chinese pick me out of the water that night. And lastly, myself, on the stand under oath, subject to all the questions that trial counsel, his staff, and the court could muster.

As we talked, I sensed Scott's lack of assurance. The background witnesses would be all right; they would serve the purpose they were designed for. It was on my testimony that the case would be won or lost, and that worried Scott. He didn't know what it could or would be. And I couldn't tell him. I wasn't sure myself. I knew that whatever it was, it would be true, and Scott knew that. But I still didn't know what it would consist of. I was glad when the meal was over, and Scott drove me back to my quarters. We didn't talk much except in generalities about the weather. I must have seemed ungrateful after all he had done, but there was nothing more I could tell him.

This time I was glad to get back to my room, to try to think and remember, for Scott's sake as well as my own. I lay down on the bed, closed my eyes, and tried to will myself back into a prison cubicle in Korea. I tried for what seemed like an hour, but it was futile. Too many other things swarmed through my mind.

Technically, I was guilty; of that, I lost all doubts. In the letter of the law, I had given aid, comfort, and support to the enemy. The broadcast was irrefutable; the other things -- the propaganda I had read, the lectures I endured -- were, although mute in court, nevertheless damning in my mind. The details -- the overcoat, the picture, even Slade -- I could explain. But the two things that mattered, the broadcast and the brainwashing, I couldn't justify, least of all to myself. Even technical acquittal was useless unless I could explain to myself what right I had to be weak. Without that, win or lose, I was condemned to know I was weak. Acquittal would be futile without justification because I would still have to live with myself. I couldn't let myself lean on Jean and forget; I had to be free in my mind.

My room was almost dark; the late-summer day that I'd anticipated with so many mixed emotions was almost over, and I was still no nearer the answer that I'd half-hoped would come out of the court martial than I'd ever been. Again for a moment I was tempted to call Jean. I compromised by getting up and looking at her picture for a moment as I lit a cigarette and then allowed myself the still almost unbelievable luxury of nibbling at a half-eaten chocolate bar. The smoke flavored the candy rather oddly but pleasantly, I thought, as I turned to look out the window. A few lights were on in the B.O.Q. opposite, and intermittent shadows were visible behind drawn shades. After a minute or two I put out the cigarette and lay back down on the bed.

A light, rapid knock on my door startled me. I sat up quickly and as I pulled the string to the overhead light, I called out "Come in." I thought it must be Scott, and I swung my feet to the floor. As I sat up, the door opened and a young man in khaki trousers and T-shirt stepped into the room. I had seen him before, a young second lieutenant who lived down the hall.

"Sir," he said, "There's a lady downstairs in the lounge. She'd like to see you," he added after an awkward pause.

He stood there, apparently waiting for a reply, uncertain whether or not one was coming. I felt momentarily sorry for him; he was too young to realize yet that colonels, too, are human in spite of silver eagles; they, too, have their fear of inadequacy. Suddenly then the impact of his words struck me.

"I'll be right down. Thank you," I said as I got to my feet.

He stepped out into the hall and then paused until I preceded him, but I hardly noticed. It had to be Jean; of that I was sure. But why had she come? Our weeks together prior to my arrest had been strained, to say the least, and even when she gave me her trust and her love, I couldn't accept them. She had been hurt in a way that only a woman could know, and yet she had come. I ran down the steps and turned into the lounge. Jean was looking out the window, her trim back toward me. I stopped suddenly, and she turned around.

"John," she said uncertainly and then walked toward me, stopping a few feet away. My eyes almost devoured her smooth, girlish face, her brown, curly hair with the light sprinkling of gray that gave it blond highlights, her moving, soundless lips, the tenseness of her eyes.

"I had to come, John," she said quietly.

I didn't know what to say. I had wanted her to come badly enough; I needed the calm reassurance of her voice and her presence, and yet I was afraid. Reassurances was not enough to rid my mind of the fear of myself that haunted it. Jean stepped closer to me then.

"You knew I wanted you to," I heard myself saying. Then almost as though I were talking to a stranger: "Would you like to sit down?"

She smiled then, as easily as she did everything.

"No, John, I think I'd rather walk. Out somewhere in the open, where we can be by ourselves. I mean completely, without . . . " She glanced around the room at the functional furniture, and continued. ". . . . the army or formality or anything. Just the two of us."

"I'm confined to my quarters," I said somewhat stiffly.

"You're a colonel. You won't run away." A shadow of a laugh crossed her face. It was contagious. I turned toward the door, smiling back in spite of myself.

We walked slowly down the gravel path past the row of B.O.Q.'s, stark, ungainly buildings that loomed against the faint ribbon of light in the western sky. Jean took my arm, but neither of us spoke until we reached a wide, tree-strewn area where I had seen occasional deer, driven out of the hills by practice gunfire, stand nervously alert. Jean looked up at me then.

"Shall we abandon the path?"

We turned and walked out into the field, through the thick yielding grass that smelled and felt clean after the gritty dust of the path. Away from the lights of the buildings, the stars seemed brighter and somehow nearer. After the heat of the day, the night air seemed almost chilly. Jean walked closer to me, and I could almost feel the tensions and fear and vivid memories of everything leave me like dreams in the morning sun. Occasionally Jean looked up at me as we walked along. We sat down as if by mutual consent. I took out cigarettes and we lit them, watched the match flare up and then out. Then Jean put her hand in mine.

"You'll go on the stand tomorrow, John," she said quietly.

"I suppose so. The prosecution rested today."

"You will. I talked to Scott on the phone."

"I wish he'd told me," I said, inhaling slowly.

"What are you going to tell them?"

"What can I tell them?" The truth. As much as I can."

"What is the truth, John?"

"I pleaded not guilty."

"What does that mean?"

"It means that the burden of proof is on the government."

"You don't mean that, John." She took her hand away and turned to face me.

"Then why did you ask?"

"You don't know what the truth is, do you?"

I felt a sudden surge of anger and threw my cigarette away. "No, I don't, if that's what you want me to say. I don't know what the truth is. I've been trying to find out. And so has the government. Or maybe they do know. God knows I don't."

"Would you know the truth if you saw it?"

I didn't answer; there was no need to. I never had and I never would. I wasn't sure that truth, universal or particular, existed. That's why I stayed in the army. That's why I went to the Mass on that Christmas Eve. If I had been sure, I'd be respectably dead like most of the regiment. But I wasn't sure, so I had gone to that Mass because it was Christmas and because I was trying to see something beyond the immediate.

"John, certain things happened during that. . .that mess. I won't ask you what they were. That doesn't matter. But you had reasons for what you did. And for what you said. I heard the broadcast, John. A newspaper reporter brought me a record and watched while I listened and then wrote a minute description."

"Jean, I . . . I didn't know that," I said, surprised.

"That doesn't matter either. What matters is what you said. And it was true. It was true then and it is now. You asked why we couldn't act like human beings instead of dogs, why we couldn't respect men's bodies and their minds instead of quarreling over them like bones. Isn't that true, John? Don't you still believe that?"

"I had no right to let myself be used."

"But were you, John? Did they use you?"

"Of course they did. Why else would they broadcast it?"

"Did you accept any of their ideas? Political or economic, that is?"

"No."

"Did you broadcast anything like that? Or sign any of the petitions or confessions they were collecting?"

"Of course not."

"Where did you get the ideas that you broadcast then? That you directed at me because you knew I would understand whatever it was that was eating away inside you?"

"I . . . I don't know. From them. Where else?"

111

"No, you didn't. I've known you too long, John, to believe that. So many times you told me the same things, the same wrongs. And you were just as angry then. But you were a soldier, an officer, you couldn't say what you thought, so those things were buried somewhere in your mind. And finally they burst out. And you say they used you! No, John. If anything, you used them. You said what you had to."

"It was for them, wasn't it?"

"No, it was for everybody. Anybody who thinks otherwise didn't listen to the words or didn't understand them. Or didn't want to understand them because they were true."

I lit another cigarette. "It would be nice if I could believe it, really wonderful; integrity, honesty, all that sort of thing is involved; I used them. I, a POW like thousands of others, used the Reds to say what I really believed. And you think I can accept that." Suddenly I laughed. "They pounded their ideas into me for months and then they used me. It was as simple as that, and that's what I'll tell them."

"That's what you want to believe, isn't it, John? That's what the prosecution believes and they've impressed it so firmly into your own mind that you want to believe it, too. You, of all people, should be able to see it for what it is."

"What do you mean by that?"

"Just plain brainwashing, John. The Reds have no monopoly on it; you've been in the army long enough to realize that. The same idea, repeated over and over, with the proper tone of authority, until its acceptance becomes second nature, until you can't even believe your own senses and your own mind anymore, or if you do, you can't do anything about it. You have to wait for the word. I've been around the army long enough to see it for what it is, too, John. Twenty years

112

now. Remember?" She stood up and looked off toward the barracks lights beyond the grove of trees. After a moment she turned to me.

"You should know, John. You went to the Point." There was more bitterness in her voice than I'd ever heard before and I was glad I couldn't see her face. She looked at me for a moment and then she turned away. "I'm going home, John. Back to the apartment."

I started to get up, but she said "Stay here, John. I can find my way. I've been trying for years." She turned to me again. "Don't let them use you tomorrow. No matter what, don't let them. I'll be at home." She turned again then and walked away in her short, rapid steps. I watched her small form, silhouetted larger than life against the nightglow in the sky until she disappeared in the dark. I stared after her long after she was gone. Finally my cigarette burned my fingers. I threw it away.

It would be nice to believe; there was no question of that. For a moment the eagles had slipped off my shoulder and I spoke what I thought; the Reds were a tool. Unconsciously, half-dead as I was, I had taken advantage of their lack of understanding of a man's conscience. I, a free man in my mind, had spoken in words they couldn't understand: the language of human compassion. That was what Jean would have me believe; that was what I wanted to believe, but something was missing, something that would let me believe it.

My burned fingers started to throb. I licked them with my almost-dry tongue and the pain eased for a moment. Then I remembered the piece that was missing. It began to form in my mind.

The broadcast was over; it had been made from my cubicle in the prison hospital, and as the Chinese radio technician took the microphone from my hands and began to roll up the cord, the three Chinese officers who had stood discretely aside, gathered around my bed. One of them started to shake my hand. In spite of the mixture of Chinese and English, their approval was obvious. I pulled my hand away. I was very tired and my head throbbed, and I wanted them to leave. In spite of the pain that made me close my eyes, in spite of the unreality of the room and the Chinese gathered around, in spite of the impossibility of my voice going beyond the room, I suddenly realized that it had. And now the Reds were congratulating me! In that moment I wanted to die.

Their voices dropped then; they started to speak in Chinese exclusively. I was glad I couldn't understand what they said. The sound of men removing the archaic radio equipment, the shuffle of feet and the scrape of heavy boxes on the floor, and over all, the high-pitched voices made me want to scream. I pleaded in my mind for oblivion: permanent, soundless, airless, lightless, thoughtless oblivion.

Suddenly there was a heavy crash and then an outburst of sing-song anger. I opened my eyes involuntarily. Someone else was in the room, talking rapidly in Chinese to the three officers. Then he turned to me. I recognized him then, an Australian, a newspaper man who made no secret of his Communist faith.

"Well, Yank, I suppose I must congratulate you. I heard your broadcast."

I closed my eyes again; I didn't want to listen.

"I told them I should have written your talk, but they wouldn't listen. Perhaps they will after this."

One of the Chinese said something then. I wanted to put my hands over my ears, but I was too tired to move.

"You were clever, Colonel. That I must admit. To pretend to cooperate and then to broadcast not propaganda designed to discourage but to make your people angry enough to want to win in order to feed, mother, take care of the world. Righteous anger. The most powerful weapon in the world if you can use it. And these fools were too blind to see it and too suspicious to let me see it for them."

I didn't understand what he meant; the words pounded into my mind, but I couldn't put them together in my mind to make sense. After a moment he went on.

"Let's hope that your people are as blind as these blokes are, that they look for the obvious answer."

And they had. All at once it was clear. Only two people of all who had heard it listened to the words. Only Jean and a Communist correspondent had seen through the situation to the truth. And now I saw it, too. I got up quickly from the bench and walked across the field, the tired heaviness gone from my body. I knew I could go into the court, face the board of officers and raise my hand. Then I could tell the truth, the whole truth, because I knew it now. And afterward, no matter what the technical verdict might be, I would be free. No matter how long it would take me to get home, Jean would be waiting.

In the Context of Life

CARTHAGE REVISITED

Ralph Gordon paid the Arab driver of the decrepit cab the requested fare even though he knew it was exorbitant and then, after a moment, added a tip that was absurdly large. He returned the man's grinning half-salute and then watched the vehicle lurch out into the street, narrowly missing a brown urchin who made the traditional hand on arm gesture at the cab. Then the boy turned and grinned at Gordon, as if to say that it was merely part of the ritual. Gordon returned the grin, and the boy darted away.

Gordon stood on the corner a moment, feeling lost. The journey that he'd started with such eagerness and satisfaction three weeks before had suddenly faded into empty anti-climax before it was over. When he left Tunis an hour and a half before, he knew where he was going, and he told the cab driver to take him directly to the monastery, but somewhere during the journey, as they passed the old German cemetery with its fading Maltese crosses crumbling after twelve years of sun and rain, he knew that his return had been too fast, that he couldn't ignore ten years of his life as easily as he'd thought. So he told the driver to take him right into Carthage instead. From there he could see the monastery on its hill, the white buildings dominating the bay and the town. He could have something to eat, and a drink or two, and do the thinking he'd neglected to do in rushing across half of America, the Atlantic, and then France and the Mediterranean. He wasn't sure why he'd come, except that after Diane left him, he had to. Now he was afraid he'd been a fool. But he still wasn't sure.

He was glad that it was May, he thought, as he stood there. If he'd waited a month or two as he'd thought he would at first, the heat would have been enough to convince him. But May was pleasant in Tunisia, almost the only comfortable time of year. He lit a cigarette and then turned away to look for one of the cafes he remembered lining the street opposite the quay, with the Bay of Tunis and Cape Bon in the foreground and the monastery off somewhere behind them, hidden from view by the buildings of the town, where its cool quiet appearance wouldn't influence his thoughts. But he'd carried the image in his mind for so long that he was sure the memory of it, more than anything else, brought him back.

As he rounded the corner onto *Rue de la Quay*, he saw that the corrugated iron fronts of the cafes were drawn shut and in front of several of them chairs were piled on the sidewalk tables. He was too late for the lunch hour; obviously the siesta observed so faithfully along the Tunisian coast was in full sway. He walked along the quay, noticing that most of the shops were closed also. A few fishermen, Arabs or French, he wasn't sure which, were mending their nets, and far off behind them, beyond the brilliant blue of the sea, the rocks of Cape Bon hulked in the sun. He passed an Arab woman tightly muffled in white. Her eyes looked sullenly at him, and he looked away.

He knew it was futile to wander about aimlessly, but there was nothing else unless he went on to the monastery. Somehow, though, he couldn't do that. The certainty that had buoyed him up for so long was gone, and all that he was sure of was that he wasn't sure of anything anymore. So he walked along until he came to the end of the quay. He had a choice. He could turn to the right and go back to the main street, he could retrace his steps along the quay, or he could stand there staring out to sea. Flicking his cigarette into the water, he turned to the right and walked slowly down the narrow, sunswept path between the white buildings.

The street was deserted, and he felt more alone than he had in a long time -- three months to be exact, when he locked the door of the hotel room behind him and unpacked the things he'd thrown into a grip, and then sat there staring at the walls, knowing that Diane had been right when she said that there was nothing between them any more, that their marriage was washed up, and that they were both intelligent enough to realize it. It was then that he knew he'd been alone for a long time, even though he hadn't realized it. He'd sat in the room for an hour, trying to remember where things had gone wrong, and then he'd gone out to get drunk. But he didn't. Instead he remembered the white buildings on the hill and knew that he'd wanted to go back for a long time. After he met Diane, he'd forgotten for a while, but the Diane phase of his life was over as suddenly as it began, and he still wanted to go back.

He came to the head of the street and turned again to his right, glancing in the few shop windows, walking slowly, knowing that if he had a camera hanging around his neck, he'd be the image of an American tourist, going nowhere, but going with determination. Or if Diane was hanging on his arm, giving little squeals of delight at the intricate Arab metal work in the windows . . .

He stopped suddenly, mentally cursing himself for thinking it. He'd put her out of his mind and his life in the three months since she'd gone to Reno, and he couldn't let her in now. He had to think, to figure out why he had come here and what he was going to do. Diane had confused him long enough. That phase was over. He couldn't let himself go back to her in his mind because he could never go back in the flesh. Neither she nor her new husband would appreciate it. He smiled at his joke.

A low, somniferous chant broke into his mind; he was nearing the market, normally the busiest, liveliest place in the town, but now, in midafternoon, almost deserted. A few women stood in front of one of the stalls. At the other stalls the merchants dozed quietly, instantly coming to their feet as he passed. He ignored the animate pleas to purchase, shaking his head slowly, knowing that with them, too, it was part of the ritual of life. The "Okay, Joe" they had learned during the war rang in his ears.

As he reached the end of the row of stalls, he saw a cafe that was open. The tables in front were unoccupied, but the corrugated iron front was rolled up, and in the dim interior, people were sitting. A serving girl scurried about. He went in, suddenly feeling tired, and sat at a table just inside where he could look out on the street. When the girl came, he ordered cognac. After the girl brought it, he settled back in his chair and lit a cigarette. He hadn't drunk cognac in almost ten years, and he looked at the glass for a moment. He didn't remember how it tasted.

Finally he picked up the glass and drank the cognac quickly, scarcely tasting it, conscious only of the sensation of being lost, feeling that he was right back where he started three months before when Diane had walked out on him, or technically, since he left the house, he had walked out on her. And now he was five thousand miles away trying to go back ten years into a past that he wasn't sure had even existed except in his own mind. As the girl came past again, he ordered another cognac.

In spite of the fact that he'd spent months in the vicinity of Carthage, had walked its streets hundreds of times, and had drunk vino in the cafes, had swum in the bay, had laid women in the dim interiors of at least a dozen of the houses, he was a stranger and he knew it. He was on the outside, looking in, looking for something that hadn't existed except that he wanted it to. He had traipsed five thousand miles on the strength of what he remembered of half an hour's conversation one night more than ten years before.

He'd been drunk that night, as he usually was in those weeks between the fall of Tunis and his unit's embarkation for Sicily. Drinking for most of the men who sat there waiting, including himself, was more than just an effort to pass time and to show the world that they were tough, unfeeling fighting men. It was an effort to fill or, failing that, to hide an emptiness deep inside themselves. But drinking didn't help; he didn't know that then, but he did now. He knew, too, that nothing filled that emptiness; you carried it with you, hoping that somehow, with drinking or a woman, or many women, or an idea that you carried in your head, you could fill it. But you never could. And here he was, at thirty instead of twenty, still trying, still knowing that it couldn't be done. He should have got drunk the night Diane left him. That would have been no more useless than his journey.

Still he remembered the conversation with one of the nameless men from the monastery up on the hill. In the course of his time in the area, he'd seen the place hundreds of times; he knew, somehow, that the order of priests who occupied it were engaged in excavating the ruins; he knew that they were trying to reconstruct some semblance of order out of the chaos and debris left by a long-gone empire. But he'd never gone up the hill. The white buildings were just something you glanced at on your way into town.

Somehow one afternoon he missed the company truck into town, and he was faced with an evening of wandering around the bivouac or lying on his bed roll in the tent with nothing to do except stare at the canvas walls and think. Rather than that, he decided to start out to walk. Once away from the area it wouldn't be hard to catch a ride into Carthage, or even into Tunis, although in Tunis, the best places were not only off limits, they were also too well patrolled by the military police. Carthage was less restricted because there were fewer troops in that area.

Outside the gate he bought a bottle of what the Arab boy claimed was cognac, and he set off, knowing that the bottle under his arm was far more effective than a raised thumb for securing a ride. When he was out of sight of the post, he walked along slowly, taking occasional sips of the cognac and glancing at the trucks or jeeps that went by. After an hour or so of walking, he decided to sit on a concrete culvert; sooner or later someone would pick him up. He was beginning to feel the effects of the cognac, and he thought that it really didn't matter whether he got into town or not, except that he was alone and it was beginning to get dark. He'd been warned often enough not to wander around alone at night. Too many G.I.'s were found beaten up or dead, with their shoes and their wallets gone. After seven months of the campaign in the interior, it would be an ironic way to get it. But he wasn't sure whether the irony would be directed at the army or himself. Anyway, it would be funny. He was sure that someone somewhere would get a good laugh out of the situation even if neither he nor the army did.

It was chow time, he knew, and traffic along the road was almost non-existent except for vehicles going the wrong way. Occasionally one of the drivers would wave at him, and he'd wave the bottle in return. His sips of the cognac were becoming more frequent, and after a while he remembered starting to walk, pausing for a while to carry on an animated conversation with himself, and then walking on, once or twice falling flat on his back in the dust along the road. Finally he dropped the bottle and wandered away from the road. Far off he heard someone blow a shrill whistle. He was tangled among grape vines, and he couldn't find his way back to the road. He kicked at the vines that he was tangled in, and then he fell flat on his face. Someone was still blowing the whistle. He tried to get up, but couldn't, and he sank into the mass of twisted vines, unable to get free.

He remembered voices talking in a language he couldn't understand, and then someone picking him up and carrying him a long way over uneven ground. The movement made him sick, and he vomited. He knew he should be afraid, but he was too miserable to care what happened. He tried to close his eyes and ignore the twisting motion, but most of it was inside him. Suddenly he knew he was in a building; he was put down on a couch. Bright light blinded him, and he closed his eyes.

Finally he awoke, conscious only of a sharp, steady pain in his stomach. He was afraid he was going to be sick again, but as he struggled to his feet, the pain eased. A man in a white robe was sitting at a table reading a book. He looked up and smiled at Gordon.

"I thought you would rest easier here than out in the vineyard. And the vines will, also." He closed his book and put it down.

Gordon didn't answer for a moment, but looked around the room. The smooth walls were painted white, and the couch, the table, and a few straight wooden chairs were the only furniture. He looked again at the man in white. "Where am I?" he asked.

"That is the usual question for one in your position," the man smiled again. His English was perfect, but the words sounded forced as he spoke them. "You are on the monastery grounds, in what is called, I believe, the gatehouse. Our Arab watchman and I carried you here after you fell among the grapes. You were, ah, ill, I believe." He paused a moment. "You are still unsure. Everything is all right except the vines that you ruined." He shook his head slowly. "Soldiers."

"I guess I didn't know what I was doing. I didn't mean to."

"Part of the hazard of being young and a soldier. It's all right. There was no lasting damage. You were among the newer vines."

Gordon's head began to ache, and the nausea returned. He sat down on the couch, feeling weak. The man's smile was making him uncomfortable, and he looked at the glaring bulb hanging from the ceiling. It hurt his eyes, and he looked back at the man, still feeling sick. He forced a smile in return.

"I'll get going. Sorry to trouble you like this."

"You needn't hurry. It's so seldom I talk to soldiers anymore. And I find them interesting. A new war, the same problems, the same answers. I was a soldier once, before you were born."

Gordon got up. "I'd better get going. Thanks for everything." He knew that if he didn't get some air, he was going to be sick. And the last thing he wanted was to talk to anyone. He'd heard it all before so many times, anyway. "Thanks a lot," he said again.

"You owe me no thanks. I was thinking of my vines. Rather I thank you and the rest of your army. A month ago German artillerymen had a gun in my vines. And they occupied this building. Any damage you did was nothing compared to theirs."

"We stick guns in people's gardens, too." He still felt uncomfortable although the nausea was lessening, and his head was still aching. He looked around for the door. It was over beyond the table, and he started to move slowly toward it, still aware of the man smiling at him. He felt he was being laughed at.

"I know that you're suffering, my friend. The night air will clear your head. But some milk will do more for the pains in the stomach. I have some here, if you would like it." He pointed to a small earthen jug standing near the door.

"No, thanks. I'd better be getting back anyway."

"First, the milk. And it does help, I know." He turned away and picked up the jug. Gordon noticed a thin black cord knotted around the man's waist. A heavy cross hung from it, swinging freely as he bent over. He turned to a cupboard behind him and took out a mug. Returning to the table, he poured it full of milk. Gordon stood there, his hand on the doorlatch. He hadn't tasted milk in almost a year, and he knew that it would ease the turmoil inside him.

"It's very good," the man said then, holding the mug out to him. He hesitated a moment and then took it from the man. It felt cool to his touch.

"Thanks," he said and sipped it. The liquid took some of the dry thickness out of his mouth and throat, and he drank deeply for a moment, feeling the coolness reach his stomach, soothing the pain and nausea. In a moment he drank it all and then looked at the mug in his hand for a moment. "It's really good," he said, putting it down on the table. "Thanks."

"Would you like some more?" the man asked, raising the jug again. "It's much better than the poison these street merchants sell for cognac." Without waiting for Gordon's answer he filled the mug again and handed it to him.

"How did you know about that?" he asked as he took it.

"I was a soldier once, as I said, and now I am a member of the White Fathers. It was not an unknown occurrence in 1916 and from my studies here at Carthage I am led to believe that it was not unknown among soldiers a thousand years ago. And when I saw what you did to my vines. . ." The man shrugged. "It was elementary, as Mr. Holmes used to say."

Gordon didn't answer. He was drinking again, enjoying the taste of the milk. He felt almost relaxed inside, and the coolness was easing his headache. Still he had the feeling that the man was laughing at him as he put down the empty mug.

"I didn't know you were a priest," he said to cover his discomfort. "I've noticed the monastery sometimes, going past. It looks nice, kind of pleasant up there on the hill."

"Pleasant? Yes, a good word, I think. We work and we pray." He smiled again. "Sometimes when we are, as you say, on the trail of something hot, we work more than we pray, but it is the same in the end. You have perhaps visited our excavations?"

"No, I haven't. I didn't know you did anything but pray."

"Work is a prayer, if it is worthwhile. We think ours is. We have a museum and a library and shops where we reconstruct what we can of the past." He sighed heavily and then smiled again. "There is so much of the past that is meaningless, and sometimes the present also. We try to make order out of that debris we dig out of the earth. Sometimes in doing so we find meaning in the present. Or at least we find it is not as meaningless as we thought when we were young." He coughed slightly. "Forgive me. I am talking too much. You would like some more milk?"

"No thanks. I had plenty. But you weren't talking too much. It just sounds different. I'm not sure I know what you mean."

"It is the talk of an old man who has been happy. Forgive me. I will call the watchman. He can show you the way to the road." He coughed again. "I am afraid I have been giving you what is called in America the commercial. But when I see a young soldier like yourself, drinking because he is sick inside without knowing why, I see myself before I came here. And I want to tell them what I have learned. But a man must learn for himself, I know. That is why I talk too much." He smiled again and moved toward the door. "I will call him."

Suddenly Gordon thought of the long walk back to the bivouac and the row of tents with their dark canvas walls, and the men in the latrines, playing cards, reading, writing letters home, in the latrine because there was no place else that had light enough. And here it was light, and the walls were bright, and the man's voice had a soothing quality like the cool milk. He wanted the man to go on talking.

"You were in the French Army before you became a priest?"

"The Austrian army actually, but it makes no difference. A soldier is a soldier. You find it strange to think that a soldier could become a priest?" He motioned Gordon to sit down.

Gordon nodded as he sat down on one of the wooden chairs.

"No more than did I, until I came here. A soldier and then a bitter ex-soldier in a defeated, impoverished land where nothing mattered, and then here." He sat silent for a moment. "First, my friend, I found work. I came here as a worker, digging in the earth for a few centimes a day. Hard, ignoble work with a pick and a shovel and the old abbe," he chuckled briefly and then went on, "who could have been at home in the galleys, using a whip, behind us, urging us on. And then one day, at the end of my shovel I found beauty, deep in the earth. A mere fragment of a pottery bowl. And then other fragments until I had form and utility and beauty there in my hands. And later, quite naturally, I found faith. Now I am here, while my old comrades and their sons are trampling Europe under their boots." He smiled at Gordon again and fell silent.

After a moment he went on, seemingly talking to himself. "Young soldiers have a right to drink. They have so little else. But it is futile to exercise that right when the very earth they dig in to shelter themselves holds so much."

There was much more that the man told Gordon, about the monastery and the life of the men who lived there, and their museum, but Gordon hardly heard the words. Instead he was living it in his mind, just as he had lived it so many times since, after he left Tunisia and went into Sicily and Italy and then finally home. Most of all he remembered the man's last words. "Come back whenever you choose, my friend. An old man likes to talk. I am called Father Wilhelm. And sometimes, when the digging goes hard, the old sergeant," he said as they shook hands.

For a long time he had intended to go back. As the landing craft pulled out of the Bay of Tunis on the way to Sicily, he watched the white buildings on the hill until they disappeared into the haze, knowing he would see them again. But as time went on, they receded still further in the haze. By the time he met Diane the memory was no more than a dream, and the old man a shadow deep in his mind. Once he had tried to talk to Diane about it, but she laughed. It was nonsense, a wish to return to the womb. Diane knew a great deal about such things. She had majored in psychology and was extremely sensible.

And now he was back in Carthage, chasing the dream of half-remembered, half-understood conversation of more than ten years before. Looking for something that he knew didn't exist. Sitting in a bar with a half-empty glass in his hand because he was afraid to go further and prove to himself that he was a fool. Doing the drinking he should have done that night Diane walked out on him so that she would finally be out of his system. Diane wasn't worth any more than that; he'd known for a long time that she had no more than a pretty face and a perfect, skillful body, commodities that she knew how to use to fulfill her wants. And she wanted far more than he had been able to give, even if she did brag to their friends that they were perfectly adjusted sexually. He drank the rest of the cognac and signaled for another.

There were three saucers on the table in front of him--three cognacs consumed. When there were five on the pile he would leave and go home. He had allowed himself to be a fool long enough; he had indulged his whim if that was what it was. Now he would be sensible and go back to Tunis. The next day he would be on a plane. In many ways Diane knew him better than he knew himself. She said he had never grown up. He would be forever a child, leaning on her and on talkative old men, showing no more intelligence than a boy. But from now on, things would be different. In a way, his trip wasn't in vain. Now he knew he was a fool. He would forget the past and go back. He had come to Carthage looking for something that he never found in Diane, and now he knew what it was. He found that he was a fool. Diane was never a fool. Many other things, but never a fool.

The bar girl put the drink in front of him, but he didn't want it. He didn't need it. He'd had enough to see things clearly. Diane wasn't worth getting drunk over, and neither was he. They had been a good pair while it lasted. And then they had done the sensible thing. They were both intelligent enough to know that. Except that he was a fool. He laughed out loud at the incongruity. Ignoring the faces that looked at him, he picked up his drink. When he put it down, the glass was empty, and he added the saucer to the little pile in front of him.

He should feel disappointed, he knew, but he didn't; he was no more disappointed than when Diane walked out on him, because in both cases, he knew the inevitable, even though he refused to recognize it until the very end. In this case, however, not quite the very end. At least he'd had sense enough not to go directly to the monastery itself.

Turning to look for the barmaid, he noticed a couple at the next table. The man's back was toward him, but the woman was staring at him rather obviously, over the man's shoulder, and there was something familiar about her. He knew it was impossible that he knew her, but her staring annoyed him. Deliberately he looked beyond her and caught the attention of the girl. He turned and looked again at the saucers, almost feeling the woman's eyes on his back. In a minute the girl brought his drink. This was the last one, he told himself as he took it off its saucer. He was perfectly sober, and he wanted to remain that way. As he took a tentative sip of the cognac he knew that wasn't quite true. This would have to be the last one, or he wouldn't be sober.

Someone touched him on the shoulder as he put the glass down.

Turning, he saw a man smiling tentatively at him. Beyond him was the woman, still staring, the shadow of a smile touching her lips.

"Good evening," the man said stiffly in English. "My wife and I would be pleased if you would join us for a drink."

"I would like to, thanks, but I'm afraid this is my last. I'm heading back to Tunis very shortly. I'm sorry."

The man shrugged his shoulders slightly. "My wife seldom finds an opportunity to talk to her countrymen here in Carthage."

Gordon smiled. "Is it that obvious?"

"Of course." He smiled apologetically. "Americans are distinctive, especially in a place like this. They are so few."

Behind him the woman leaned forward across the table. "Please join us," she said and then smiled. It was a full, brilliant smile, and suddenly Gordon thought of Diane. He tried to put her out of his mind, but the woman continued to smile. The image of Diane forced its way into his mind again, and he looked at his glass in an effort to drive her away

"Until I finish this one," he said evenly as he rose. Inwardly he felt in a turmoil, angry at himself for agreeing and for thinking of Diane. He picked up his drink and turned to the other table.

The woman indicated the chair beside her, and he sat down. In a moment the man sat down opposite. He was about forty-five, and seemed tired or much older, Gordon decided. There were heavy lines in his face, and his hair was almost entirely gray.

The woman touched Gordon's arm lightly. "You must forgive me for being so insistent, but I almost never see Americans any more. We've been here three years." She smiled again.

"It's all right," Gordon said. "I understand." He studied her a moment, noticing again that she did seem familiar. She was about thirty-five, he decided, and the smile that she turned on and off so easily and effectively reminded him of Diane. And even more remarkable was the set of her face when she wasn't smiling. It might have been cast in the same mold as Diane's. And not only Diane's, he reflected, but also the countless faces that stared out from the smooth pages of the better-class American magazines. He felt sorry for the man.

They exchanged names then, and he shook hands with the man. He was surprised at the firmness of the man's grip. While they made the usual inconsequential comments that people make on such occasions, he regretted that he hadn't refused their invitation. It was only more evidence that he was a fool, he thought, as the man ordered a bottle of cognac. When it was brought, the woman insisted upon pouring a few drops into his glass although it was almost full. She stopped pouring skillfully as the liquid touched the brim.

"You can't leave Carthage without having one drink with me," she said. Gordon noticed her use of the singular, just as Diane often did, as she went on. "I suppose you are a salesman. Most Americans who find their way here are selling something or other. In fact, it seems as though all

Americans are salesmen of sorts. Earnest, sincere, hardworking salesmen." She looked at her husband for agreement. He was pouring himself a drink and didn't respond.

"No, I'm not a salesman," Gordon said. "I've never been able to sell anything. According to your definition I suppose I'm not much of an American." He was annoyed at her remark and didn't mind showing it.

"Have you been here before? In Carthage, I mean." She asked.

"Yes, once. A long time ago."

"During the war?"

"Yes."

"And now you've returned. Byronic."

"Hardly that. More accidental than anything, I guess."

They didn't speak for a moment. The woman sipped her cognac quickly and refilled her glass from the bottle. Gordon felt annoyed. In her oblique way she seemed to be trying to hand him his conversational cues, and he felt that she, too, was annoyed at his replies. He sipped again at his drink and turned to her husband.

"I hardly expected to find Americans here in Carthage."

"My wife is the American. I am German," he replied stiffly, giving Gordon the impression that he had been expected to make the distinction himself. The man smiled apologetically then, and Gordon felt like an intruder.

"My husband is a salesman," the woman said. Her voice sounded metallic. "The Germans are also good salesmen. They are much like the Americans in that respect, only more so. They are too serious."

"My wife dislikes salesmen," the man said and then sipped at his drink. He put the glass down on the table and stared at it. "Salesmen are such petty creatures; they are not worthy of the notice of an artist." He picked up his glass again and sipped the cognac.

"I have never said that," the woman said suddenly.

"You don't have to use words directly," the man said.

The woman looked at Gordon then. She had leaned forward in her chair and there was an odd light in her eyes. It seemed as though she had moved closer to him although her chair hadn't moved. "My husband finds art trying and insignificant." She smiled at Gordon and then looked down at his hands. "Do you paint?"

"No." Gordon tried to think of an excuse to leave.

"Or write?"

"I've tried. Not very hard or very well, though." He decided he would have to be polite until he finished his drink.

"You should go on with your writing. You have the hands of an artist."

Gordon didn't reply; instead he sipped at his drink, determined to finish it and then leave as he'd said he had to.

"Yes, you should write," the woman went on. "The act of creation is important, the only really important thing in life."

"I suppose it is, if one has the talent and the ambition," Gordon replied.

"My wife finds it very absorbing," the man said, pouring himself another drink. "It gives her the strength to endure salesmen."

"You don't understand. Mr. Gordon is a writer. And he is a primitive. American writers are always primitives. He understands." She looked directly at Gordon as she spoke. He looked down at his glass, thinking again of Diane.

"You once thought I understood," the husband said mildly.

"You did, once. When you let yourself forget that you were a German businessman out to restore the reputation and fortunes of the fatherland."

"A man cannot play forever, my dear. Even the young captain in Algiers could not play forever." The corners of his mouth held the hint of a smile, but he stared out the doorway into the street.

"That was nothing. You know that was nothing," the woman said passionately. Her face was flushed under the make-up.

"And there were others who understood, were there not? Others who also felt that art is above and apart from life, forgetting that artists must eat and breathe and feel like mere men."

"That is not fair." She drank quickly from her glass, and then, leaning forward in her chair, refilled it from the bottle.

No one spoke for a few moments. They both seemed to have forgotten Gordon's presence, and the tension between them was almost tangible. Gordon picked up his glass to finish his drink; as he did so, he felt the slight pressure of the woman's knee against his under the table. He moved slightly and the man glanced at him. Then he looked back at his wife.

"You are making Mr. Gordon feel neglected, my dear. Perhaps you should tell him about your work. Or should I say your pleasure?"

"My work is my pleasure." She turned to Gordon, and he noticed a pink cast in her eyes. The cognac was showing its effect, he thought. "Mr. Gordon, as my husband suggests, I will tell you about primitive art. The only true art because it does not depend on trickery or technique. I am a primitive painter. I can tell you." She smiled a moment and then went on: "We shall ignore my husband. He does not exist. He is not a primitive. I am a primitive and you are a primitive." She held out her glass as she spoke, and her husband poured it full of cognac.

As the woman paused to taste her drink, the man filled his own glass and then handed the bottle to Gordon. Gordon noticed the man's hand shake almost imperceptibly. Then the woman put down her glass and moved her chair closer to Gordon. Gordon put the bottle down on the table without taking any cognac. The woman's smile flashed on and off, and then she spoke again.

"Yes, I am a primitive painter. Handicapped, of course, by both knowledge and training, but nevertheless a primitive by nature and by inclination. I have resolved to rid all my work of the idiotic restraints imposed by convention." She paused and took a rapid swallow of the cognac and then, with her glass in her hand, smiled at him again.

"A primitive is one who refuses to let himself be dictated to by those who set themselves up as authorities. A primitive is ruled from within, not from without. He feels, he senses, because he is free from everything that might inhibit his sensitivity. And because he is free, he is capable of creating true art."

The woman's words sounded oddly familiar to Gordon. Instead of being phrased in the psychological jargon that Diane affected, the woman used art as her catch-all, but the meaning was the same. He felt like slapping her, as he did with Diane when she started her routine, but instead, he smiled at the woman as he had so often forced himself to do before. "In other words, to be a true primitive, a person must be quite modern. Rid himself of anything that tends to warp the true expression a person is capable of." He felt almost as though he were in the living room of the apartment, deliberately and patiently avoiding a scene.

"Exactly," the woman said eagerly. "In art or in everyday life, it's all the same. A painter who is truly free can depict life because he lives it." She put her hand on his arm excitedly. "You must write again, Mr. Gordon," she said, breathing heavily.

A four-letter army expression came to Gordon's mind suddenly. It was the only word he knew that expressed his feelings completely. But once he had used the expression to Diane, and he wouldn't make that mistake again. He moved his arm out from under the woman's hand. "On that theory, perhaps the only true primitive is an ape in the jungle. He's completely ruled from within, and he's certainly capable of removing, or for that matter, destroying anything that tends to inhibit him."

She took his remark seriously. "An ape lacks intelligence. He is hardly capable of accomplishing something lasting."

"He certainly isn't handicapped by knowledge or training."

Her husband smiled at that, but the woman frowned and picked up her glass. When she put it down, it was empty. The man seemed on the point of speaking, but then he refilled her glass from the almost empty bottle. He reached over then and refilled Gordon's.

Gordon glanced at his watch significantly. "I really don't have time for another. I've got to confirm my plane reservation."

"Please, Mr. Gordon, just one more. My wife so enjoys talking with her countrymen when she has the opportunity.' He smiled tolerantly at her, but his eyes seemed cold.

"I really have to go." He glanced at his watch again.

A beggar child came up to their table then. He was covered with sores and was leading an old man whose eyes rolled sightlessness in their sockets. As Gordon glanced at them, the child held out a dirt-smudged card. It held the usual plea, Gordon knew, and he handed the child a fifty-franc note. The man did also, but Gordon noticed that the note was larger. The woman glanced briefly at the child and then looked quickly away with an air of obvious distaste. The child thanked them in gestures and led the old man to the next table.

The man sighed heavily. "It's easy to refuse to acknowledge the existence of poverty and disease if it doesn't affect -- or inhibit -- yourself."

"Yes, it is. And we're all guilty, I'm afraid," Gordon said quickly. He was determined to go immediately, and although he really sympathized with the man, he knew that it was futile to go on sitting there, talking and drinking cognac. He pushed his chair back from the table.

"Well! He looks well fed," the woman said shrilly. She was staring out the door into the street, sipping her drink.

Gordon looked out. A priest, dressed in the habit of the White Fathers, was walking by, his small round hat sitting squarely on his head as a soldier might wear it. For a sudden moment, he thought it was Father Wilhelm, but then he knew that it was unlikely at best. There were dozens in the monastery. He glanced at the woman. She was smiling triumphantly.

"Would you prefer him if he were not?" he asked quietly.

"Then he would be a fool."

It was the answer he expected. But it was pointless to go on talking, and he rose from the table, looking out into the street again. The priest walked on in a directed, determined manner, and suddenly Gordon knew what he had to do. He had to go up on the hill before he could leave Carthage. It was the only way he could determine whether that night and the man he talked to ten years before were real or a dream, the only way there was any possibility of exorcising himself of the aching void inside him that Diane and her primitive ideology had never been able to fill.

"Will you excuse me? I really have to go."

The man smiled tiredly as he nodded. The woman said nothing. As Gordon turned away, she was filling her glass. He went on out into the street. Perhaps he was a fool, but he had to find out for himself.

THE MAN OF ACTION

The little man, who had been cordial since I joined the faculty, settled back in my leather chair, casually looked at the books in the case at his elbow, and then sipped contemplatively at his bourbon and water.

"Yes, always in the fall I feel the illogical urge to return to the life of action."

"The life of action?" I inquired casually, sipping at my own drink.

"The war, that sort of thing. You know, I really enjoyed the war."

I didn't know, I informed him, expressing mild surprise. I had rather enjoyed the war, but he hardly seemed the type.

"One can set aside all moral and ethical considerations and give full reign to his destructive impulses." He sipped again idly, as though waiting for me to question him further.

Instead, I added quietly, "Or self-destructive, perhaps."

"What? Yes, perhaps that's so. I was in field artillery, a forward observer before I was given my own battery. We had the maximum opportunity for destruction, combined with the minimum amount of exposure to same, to borrow a phrase from Shaw," he went on self-consciously.

"Yes," I agreed. "I found myself envying you artillerymen at times," I went on in order to give him the opportunity to revel in the memories of what had once accidentally been and could be no more. It was his night out, and I knew that he was determined to enjoy it in approved academic and yet masculine fashion. I am not intending to construct a paradox in such a remark, and yet I felt its odd presence. "You boys certainly had the maximum opportunity for destruction."

"Yes," he said at once. "And it was not without an odd sort of humor of its own at times. I remember one afternoon in Italy, when I was on the hill.We called it 'on the hill' when we were adjusting fire, whether we were actually on a hill or not," he added and then sipped his whiskey again.

"Yes, I know," I murmured, studying him more closely in mild disbelief but carefully disguised.

"I noticed a small structure made of tree branches and covered with a bit of camouflage cloth. It occurred to me that it was probably an enlisted man's latrine. Enemy, of course."

"Of course."

"In a moment of pure whimsy I called in a fire mission, identifying it as enemy infantry in foxholes. You see, I always preferred to use proximity fuses -- fuse V.T. -- and watch the air bursts and the fragments slash through the brush."

"From a safe distance," I interjected humorously.

"Oh, yes, from a safe distance." He went on with the story, describing in an almost clinical manner but using a rather inappropriate glee: the shell bursts, the perceptible movement underneath the camouflage, and the sudden emergence of a middle-aged German private trying to pull his trousers up with one hand, and then staggering, white buttocks flashing in the sun as he jerked under another burst, fell, and lay still. It was all told with the same detached humor, much as I imagine surgeons find themselves discussing a particularly hilarious infected gall bladder or diseased kidney. I decided momentarily that perhaps I had misjudged the man from the first. But then I remembered it was his night out.

His name was Laurence Roll, and he was Professor of English at the University. I do not normally underestimate professors of English; I am one myself, and I am well aware that we are of four types, pansies who would prefer to be truck drivers, truck drivers, dilettantes, and the occasional genuine scholar who in his mild way is completely absorbed by his specialty. I am a dilettante, and Roll, I had been convinced, was a scholar. Normally his conversation centered on the Early English Romantics to the exclusion of everything else and the boredom of Restoration Drama specialists like myself.

"I'm not boring you with these war stories, am I, Peterson?" he asked as I became aware of the end of another anecdote.

"On, no, nothing like that. I'm enjoying it. I seldom think about the war anymore," I added, getting up to replenish our drinks.

"I do. Quite frequently. Louise thinks I'm a bore."

Louise was Roll's wife, and I could well imagine that she thought he was a bore. The two were badly mismated, I was sure, from a casual conversation I had enjoyed with her at a cocktail party several weeks earlier, just after school had opened. A fine-looking woman with a high, full bust and taut buttocks, she had been intriguingly but not quite perceptibly tight, and I had gently probed over the canapes. She was quite willing to talk. I knew she was bored by the Early English Romantics; she hadn't mentioned the war.

"You bachelors certainly have it over the rest of us," Roll commented as he sipped at his fresh drink. "The uninterrupted leisure for scholarship, the money for travel, and, I dare say," he added wickedly, "a certain fascination for the ladies."

I braced myself mentally for continued recitation of further anecdotes of the life of action, a different kind of action. I had been entertaining married friends on their nights out for many years. Surprisingly he turned easily to shoptalk.

"That was a fine piece of work you did on John Dryden," he commented, sipping again. "A badly-needed re-evaluation that put old Murchison in his place."

"I wasn't aware that you kept up in my field," I remarked without irony although Stanley Murchison, the renowned Dryden scholar, had been dead almost half a century.

"I don't, really, not as much as I'd like to. But I did read your book. I was on the committee that selected you, you know."

"Thank you, Larry. I shall try to deserve your confidence," I said mock-formally, although I had suspected such was the case.

"Oh, there was really no contest. When a man of thirty-eight has published as much substantial work as you have, there's little doubt as to his value. Now I suppose we older men will have to tend more closely to our knitting, keep the library fires burning, so to speak, or be left behind." He laughed self-consciously, well aware that I knew he was not quite forty-five, hardly an old man for a full professor.

He really was a pedant, I reflected, and the life of action was no more than a late adolescent interlude in what was otherwise a rather stodgy existence.

No wonder Louise was bored. I was bored myself, and I hardly knew the man.

"You've been to the Far East since the war, haven't you, Peterson?" he inquired, glancing idly at a Japanese mask on the wall opposite.

146

"Yes, twice. I did some work on the Japanese Noe drama."

"Guggenheim?"

"No, on my own. I've never felt it quite fair to take money I didn't absolutely need."

"You bachelors," he said again, shaking his head slowly. "Still, I've a sabbatical coming up year after next, and I'd toyed with the idea of going there. Louise is crazy about the possibility."

I said nothing, although I was well aware of Louise's interest in the East. There had been a chance encounter in the drugstore, a shared cup of coffee, and a lift home that I was sure Roll knew nothing of. And then there had been the considerably less formal party given by a young instructor, while Larry read early Romantic poetry to a tape recorder. And another chance encounter or two. Louise wasn't really interested in the East. She was simply bored.

"I'm not keeping you from anything, am I, Peterson?"

"Oh, no, nothing. A few papers I promised to look over for my honors students. Nothing important."

"Perhaps I'd better be getting along."

"It's quite early. Let me get you another drink."

"All right." He settled back in the chair and again let his eyes wander over the books in the case beside him. I brought the drinks, and we chatted for a while about personalities in the department, but I knew that Roll's night out, his life of action for the week, was over. Finally he finished his drink and glanced at his watch.

"It's after eleven. I'd best be getting on."

"All right." I walked with him to the door, and we exchanged goodnights. "Tomorrow night is my night to babysit," he said as he went out the door. "Perhaps you'll stop over for a drink."

"Perhaps. I won't promise." I waited a moment and then closed the door behind him. He was walking, and it would take him at least fifteen minutes to cross the campus and get home. As he rounded the corner I turned to the telephone.

Seduction has often been termed dishonorable, even nasty business, but I have never found it so. Rather I prefer to regard it as a sport, a most enjoyable life of action, to use Roll's phrase. This particular prospect interested me greatly, because I, too, was bored, and I had determined to make Louise Roll my mistress.

Actually it was not as simple as this may imply, but no more difficult than I had anticipated. I had had a number of experiences with faculty wives before. Louise was no more and no less difficult than her predecessors. However, the procedure itself was quite simple. Through a series of carefully contrived, chance meetings I made known my desires through indirection and innuendo, and by the same means I ascertained hers. They coincided, as I had anticipated. There was much talk of attraction that was quite direct and of love that was vague. I was in no hurry; I was on tenure.

I became a friend of the family, giving Louise and the children lifts to nursery school and dancing class; I joined Larry on his night out; I escorted Louise to a play while Larry graded papers and watched the children. It was all quite innocent, and in spite of the fact that 1 enjoyed my role, I kept in mind the inevitable outcome. It was a matter of more than four months.

Convincing Louise that she should spend her "evenings out" with me was no problem. She was fond of modern films, especially foreign, and the University sponsored a good series. I confessed to a similar interest, and we fell into the habit of meeting at the box office each Thursday evening for the first show. She wouldn't let me pay for her, and whether Larry knew of our meetings I have no idea. We didn't speak of them in his presence, although we occasionally discussed the films.

In the theater she was like a child, running the whole gamut of human emotions without reservation, seemingly unaware of my close observation although I was certain she knew that I watched her. In the half-light her thirty-three years disappeared, and the play of light and shadow on her face revealed the sort of innocence that almost inevitably ensnares a man of my nature. I managed to keep my emotions carefully controlled, however, revealing them only in moments of artless innuendo. She was both flattered and interested.

Then there was usually a cup of coffee at the drugstore and a bit of conversation about the films before we went our separate ways. I managed to direct the conversation into immediacies rather well, although normally I find such films and such conversations damnably dull. We carried on in this manner throughout the winter and into the early spring. It became rather tedious, and when I found myself casting inquiring glances at an attractive young graduate student and several of the more mature coeds, I realized that it was no longer a sport. My career simply could not tolerate the kind of indiscretion that I had become susceptible to.

The next Thursday there was a showing of an early Ingmar Bergman film. Louise had not seen any Bergman, and she was anticipating it keenly. I knew the film, and I knew that it could not fail to stimulate her emotions. We met at the box office.

The effect of the film was as I had anticipated: the skillfully handled unfolding of the old theme of life and love struggling against time and death left her breathless. At the conclusion I silently led her to my car, saw her inside, and then got under the wheel. Neither of us spoke until we had reached the edge of the campus.

"Well," she said, sighing deeply as she smiled at me.

"It was quite an emotional bloodbath." I looked straight ahead.

"You needn't be cynical. It was so pathetically futile."

"Is that so unusual that we be overwhelmed by it -- " I paused deliberately and then looked at her for the first time -- "in a film?"

"Of course not, silly." She touched my arm lightly, and then giggled softly. "You won't deny that it affected you as strongly as it did me."

"We are talking about the film, aren't we?"

"What else? But then I suppose you don't understand. You've never been a woman -- nor married."

I could have corrected her on the latter, but instead I said, "Is it necessary to be a woman to see one's feelings mirrored on the screen?"

"Oh, Bob." We fell into silence that lasted until I slowed the car for the drugstore corner, both of us staring straight ahead.

"Drugstore coffee seems rather inadequate after such an experience," I remarked as I pulled alongside the curb and stopped.

"Yes."

We sat there a moment, and then I looked at her again. There was a faint forced smile on the corners of her tightly-set lips.

"I could buy you a drink, you know."

"Yes. But that's impossible in this town. You know that."

"Ridiculous, perhaps, even futile, but not impossible. I have some rather good bourbon." I sounded wistful, even to myself.

"All right." I expected comments about "Perhaps just one," or "I should get right on home," but she became silent again. Without a word I drove quickly to my house and pulled into the drive. She slipped out before I could open her door.

My living room was both masculine and scholarly, and I was rather fond of it, but she didn't seem to notice her surroundings. Instead she sat on the couch, drew her legs up under her, and smiled eagerly.

"I'll have sweet soda with mine, if you have it."

"I have." I turned to the liquor cabinet, relieved that if she did feel nervous she didn't betray it. As I turned again to ask her if she preferred ice she was coming toward me. In a moment she was in my arms. I kissed her hungrily, and her lips parted, her small tongue darting like a snake striking. As my hand slip downward, she shivered, and her mouth opened wider. I wanted no mishaps, and so I held her tightly, and we explored each other's mouths.

As my lips began to ache deliciously, she pulled her mouth free. I relaxed my grip slightly.

"Bob, this is impossible. What are we doing?"

"The inevitable," I murmured, recognizing that she had to observe the formalities.

Without answering she closed her eyes, and her lips parted slightly. I moved in quickly, and our bodies strained together. After a long moment I picked her up in my arms, and her lips glided moistly to my neck. As my hand moved to the bare flesh of her thigh she quivered again and bit sharply at my skin.

After one or two more attempts we gave up the presence of enjoying the movies; each moment was too vital, and although we did manage to steal two delightful matinees we were restricted to Thursday evenings, when Larry was safely minding the children at home. There were other possibilities, of course, but my house was not quite safe at other times, motels are degrading, and I regard back-seat episodes as both adolescent and unsatisfying. In spite of the arbitrary limits imposed on our affair we both enjoyed it unreservedly, and happily it did not become messy. I had chosen well.

Of course our other activities went on normally. I was the friend of the family, chauffeuring Louise and the children to various functions, enjoying Louise's delicious roast beef at Sunday dinners and complimenting her exaggeratedly, and almost every Wednesday evening I entertained Larry. Relaxing in my huge leather chair, away from the routine of the domestic establishment, sipping my bourbon and growing expansive as he enjoyed it, he spoke occasionally with nostalgia of the life of action, while with great patience I sat through a number of recitals of his hilarious adventures as an artilleryman-murderer. I grew to like the man and I felt sorry for him, so I was willing to let him indulge himself in his moments of fantasy.

For the most part, however, we talked shop; personalities, campus and departmental politics, the tedious trivia that occupy so much time that the academic cannot spare and yet that he cannot resist wasting. On occasion he spoke of Louise, sometimes, at rare intervals, of intimacies that I knew better than he but could not discuss. Even at such times I forbore impatience. He was a likeable chap in spite of his incredible dullness.

Of Louise I cannot say too much. She was unbelievably lovely and passionate in the full bloom of her maturity. She lost all semblance of girlhood in such moments and became completely a woman. The moderation with which we were forced to approach our love made each shared moment intense, and we met with a force that was almost ferocious. Her quick thrusts, her rising tension, and her overwhelming climaxes gave me a joy that I had scarcely known before.

Such meetings left us both limp with exhaustion and satisfaction.

As we lay there afterward with the light glistening on our moist bodies, renewing our energies, I took delight in exploring her body, its mounds, its depressions. At the same time we talked desultorily.

"Have you always been so lusty, my Bob?"

"Lustful," I corrected. "When I'm with you," I murmured, gently tracing the roundness of her thigh with my fingertips.

"Lusty lustful Bob," she sighed. "And I like it -- you -- so much." Her stomach muscles tightened involuntarily under my hand, and I felt anticipation gather inside me again. My fingers moved more eagerly and more forcefully over her body. The talk was meaningless, it was nonsense, but I knew that it kept the glow of Louise's fire fanned until it should again burst into flame, so I suffered it willingly, even gladly.

It was on just such an evening that we lay there, while the late May breeze washed over our bodies from the open window and I explored easily, hardly listening to Louise's lazy remarks. Our meeting had been fraught with the full force of the spring night, and it had been almost explosive. We recouped our energies more slowly than usual; it was the intensity of our moment, the softness of the night, the reward of moderation that we savored in respite even as we anticipated reunion.

"The breeze is smoother -- stronger," she whispered lazily.

"Shall I cover you?" My hand moved toward the sheet.

"No, silly, let me enjoy it. Softly touching me." Her voice trailed off, and I lessened the pressure of my fingers.

She was close to sleep, and sleep is at its luxurious best at such moments. I continued to stroke her softly and rhythmically until I, too, was close to that epitome of sensuous slothfulness.

Just as we were both slipping into a state of somnolence the door to the room burst open, rebounding with a crash from the doorstop. Louise reached desperately for the sheet, while I opened my eyes. It was Larry. He was indeed the man of action as he stood in the doorway glaring down at us.

His open-necked shirt displayed a vein throbbing in his throat; his face was livid, and in his hand he had a huge army .45. Louise gave a small shriek as she pulled the sheet over her, and the image of a fierce little man directing fire on a German latrine passed through my mind. He stood there a moment and coolly pointed the gun at the bed. I had never experienced quite such a denouement before; both my eyes, I am sure, were wide open, and Louise moaned softly beside me.

The pistol barked sharply; the pillow between us leaped convulsively, and Larry leered through the cordite fumes.

"That was no accident," he shouted triumphantly. "I fired 'expert' with the pistol." Even then I could hear the invented commas. To punctuate his words the pillow jumped again. Louise shrieked; the noise and the fumes gave me a slight headache. I closed my eyes and waited, while Louise sobbed brokenly beside me.

"Louise, get dressed," he commanded sharply. She stirred beside me, and I opened my eyes wide enough to see her disappear into the smoke. I closed them again and continued to wait.

After a while it struck me that I was alone, and opening my eyes, I found that I was. I stared through the smoke at the wreckage of my pillow, and then got up to put on a dressing gown. It had been an exciting evening.

Later, sipping a bourbon, I reflected on the suitability of what had happened. It was spring, final examinations were in sight and an affair that had started to become old hat had run its course. And perhaps even then the committee of a department that needed a Restoration Drama man was thumbing through my work on Dryden. As I sipped again, I sighed. I had enjoyed my acquaintanceship with the Rolls.

RED BALL, OHIO

The earth had more than completed two orbits, spring had become spring again and then spring again, George Crile General Hospital had become Crile Veterans Hospital, and the gate was open, unguarded. Once more a civilian, pronounced healed, with scar tissue firmly established in the appropriate places but aching a bit, I walked almost jauntily out onto the street. Temporarily an outpatient, only temporarily totally disabled, I carried nothing with me except what we used to call an AWOL bag in basic. It was almost empty. My cheap PX suitcase awaited Railway Express, and I walked to the bus stop in bright midmorning sun, almost free.

The two tickets in my pocket, CSR and Greyhound, would take me to the Public Square in downtown Cleveland and then home, courtesy of a grateful government. I had taken the tickets, together with my release papers, my medication instructions, and my outpatient authorization without comment or questions; they were the last in a long trail of paper that began more than four years in the past, and that I hoped had come to an end. But the bus schedule on the post beside me made no sense; I had no schedule, and I began to walk again.

The war was clearly, finally over, and a steady stream of cars, a few of them shiny and new, roared past, leaving a breeze and a haze and a smell behind them. It was good to see them, hear them, smell them as I walked along the shoulder of a road not quite suburban, and I wondered vaguely where they were going. Several of them honked, one or two passengers waved, and I felt pretty good.

Ohio Route 82 at Brecksville, a mile and a half north of the hospital, was suburban, complete with Standard, Shell, Sohio, and Sunoco stations at the four corners. I was sweating slightly in my new PX suit, although the temperature hadn't yet reached 60, and I stood there, watching the light change and the cars move with orderly ease through the intersection. It was the outside, and I hadn't thought about the outside or the past or the future, both of which it was a part, for a long time; occasionally, in the past year, especially after the electricity had coursed through my brain, obliterating memories, I wasn't aware that either past or future existed. I loosened my new civilian necktie, crossed the road with the light, and began to walk west, on the north shoulder of the road, toward home.

Remembering the tickets, I was momentarily annoyed, and tearing them up, I fed them to the wake of the cars. Home was only sixty miles west, Northern Ohio was becoming spring, and no one was expecting me. I was in no hurry; for the first time in almost five years there was no place I had to be, nothing I had to do, and time had lost its meaning more than two years before. And yet I didn't know what to do; there was no one to tell me, and so I kept on walking.

Walking west, in an American tradition that seemed no older than the two years since shell fire had interrupted what seemed to be an interminable walk-crawl-stumble across Tunisia, across Sicily, across half of Italy, I began to lose myself in the fact and rhythm of the act, and my right hand, made supple again by months of therapy, began to stir itself, gradually my forefinger inscribing triangles on my thumb in the manner that had silently preserved my sanity until the commissioned shrink, obsessed with the silver eagles on his shoulders, finally gave up his probing and went home to

Brooks Brothers suits and a much more lucrative practice than broken GIs could provide.

1 had seen them come and go, from medical commissions or technical stripes to medical prosperity or peonage; I had had a brief unconsummated affair with a blond, blue-eyed nurse, but it had evaporated when she went home to California, wrote twice, and then became silent.

And now I was gone, leaving other broken ones in blue bathrobes, monogrammed US, and in GI pajamas and paper slippers behind me. The war was over and the band welcoming me to freedom was the steady drone, the occasional sharp blast of horn, the breeze tugging at my clothes as I walked steadily west on the shoulder of Ohio 82, past occasional houses set back from the road, past a line of mailboxes, past an unpaved, unnamed side road leading into distant woods, spring-dusted with green. Somewhere I had read that it was necessary for a man to touch rock bottom at least once before he could be whole, and I had touched it and remained there for longer than I could remember and I was now walking free in the sun, in a world newly green.

What was behind me -- more than four years of it -- remained with me, in grainy shades of gray, like a slightly out-of-focus, shaky eight millimeter home movie from the thirties. What was ahead didn't exist, nor would it. But shadows from the past, like old photos, tried to slip into focus somewhere in the back of my mind. Yet the electrical jolts that coursed through my head, from one Vaseline-smeared electrode to another, the new treatment, the Cadillac of treatments, the shrink told me before returning to his Brooks Brothers suit, neither erased those out of focus faces nor let me remember more than the shadows of what had been. And part of me believed that, if not good, it was just as well that I had forgotten.

A wide, well-kept lawn swept down from a new ranch-style house to the shoulder of the road in front of me. I glanced up at the house. It was like a picture, like so many of the new low, one-storied houses appearing in the advertisements and plans in the slightly used magazines brought to Crile by those who remembered us and meant well. I moved to my right, to feel the grass under my feet after what seemed like miles of gravel. As I paused and looked up at the house again, a small boy, four perhaps, towheaded, wearing a bright red jacket, materialized about ten feet away. I smiled; we saw few children in the hospital. But his face froze in a pout, and then he shouted in a near-scream: "This is my yard. Go away."

I glanced up the broad sweep of lawn again not sure how to reply. My smile faded, and I said seriously, "Nobody's going to take it away from you, kid. You can bet on that." I moved back to the graveled shoulder and walked on. But I could feel him standing there, his eyes suspiciously staring at my back.

There were children in my past, I knew, children whom I didn't frighten, children who came out of the rubble when the shelling stopped, children among the faded photos in my mind, among the photos of people, of events, of pain that, unimaginable, beyond communication, beyond recall, were there. In spite of the warmth, my sweat turned cold, and I began to walk farther and faster west, the only direction I knew. But the child, the first person of my freedom, remained with me, his frown, of fear or defiance or even hate, in clear focus against the background of shadows.

It was nearly noon, the sun high, the sweat warm again when I passed a battered sign that said "North Royalton," crossed one intersection with the light, paused briefly in front of a Standard station, feeling the dryness of my throat, and the sweat, warm again, a brief rumble in my stomach, an insistent pressure in my bladder. A nondescript tavern with its sign Beer Wine Food, a few cars, a red semi and trailer proclaiming Iron City Beer parked in front, were just down the road. And I had money -- three one-hundred dollar bills, a twenty, and some ones clipped together in my wallet, a dollar sixty subsistence in my pocket, a handful of change -- and I was free. With a sudden surge of confidence I walked across the rutted parking lot and went in. It had been a long time.

After the bright sun it was dark inside, the gloom punctured by red neon over the bar across the room. I stood there a moment, until the two or three shadows became two men hunched over the bar some six feet apart, a massive woman behind the bar, leaning on it and talking to one of the men. I walked over, selected a stool midway between the two men, dropped my bag beside it, and took off my jacket and draped it over the next stool. 1 sat down, casually but carefully. Each move had been rehearsed often enough in my mind in the days and weeks when I knew I would be free.

The woman straightened up -- she was tall as well as wide. "What'll it be, fella?" Her voice was oddly high.

"Can I get a sandwich? Or some soup?" It was as easy as I knew it would be.

"We got hamburgs, cheese burgs, ham n cheese, hot beef or baloney. And French fries. No soup."

"I'll have a hamburger. With ketchup and relish." It was even easier than I expected. I knew I could function again.

"Anything to drink?"

I flushed; I had forgotten. "And a bottle of beer. Iron City." I remembered.

The woman laughed. "We don't serve that stuff here. Got Budweiser, Schlitz, Pabst, P.O.C."

"Oh, P.O.C., I guess." I had forgotten it existed, and I wasn't sure what it was.

"Pride Of Cleveland, right." She opened the cooler under the bar.

The man to my right laughed. "Piss on Cleveland, all right. You mean Piss on Cleveland."

She laughed again. "You goddamn Hoosiers don't know what good beer is. Haulin all that stuff from Pittsburg." She opened the bottle, hit it briefly with a bar rag, and put it down in front of me in one smooth movement, and then turned and called for a "Hamburg, k and r," into a brighter window behind her.

After she put down a glass she turned back to the man beside me, murmured something, and then giggled as he replied. I poured beer carefully into my glass and tasted it. Then, suddenly, I drained the glass and emptied the bottle into it. The aftertaste, the coolness in my throat, and the slight belch all felt good. I looked around for the men's room.

It was around the end of the bar. I slid off the stool, walked carefully around, and went in, feeling for the first time familiar, knowing that I could function. The tiny room smelled musty, and it would never pass inspection, but it was on the outside. I stared at the contraceptive machine over the urinal, read Sold Solely For the Prevention of Disease and the fine print below, and then looked at my face -- clean shaven, shiny from sweat, indeterminate age, brown hair, a touch of

162

gray at my temples -- as I rinsed my hands in the dirty washbowl, shaking them damp rather than risk the towel. I looked like anybody else. Grinning with pleasure, I went back to the bar as the woman put down my hamburger beside my glass and removed the empty bottle. It all seemed new and yet familiar.

"Eighty-five cents," she said.

I pulled out my handful of change, put down a half, a quarter, and a dime and, then, remembering, put a quarter beside them. She pushed it back to me. I let it lay, momentarily confused.

"Nobody tips in this joint. It ain't allowed."

"No, you don't want to spoil 'er," the man beyond me said. "She's got enough ideas as it is."

"No, I just thought . . ." I bit quickly into the hamburger. It was moist inside, the ketchup sharp, the meat warm. I ate it quickly, washing it down with the beer.

"What's a matter, kid" Don't they feed you at Crile anymore?" The man grinned at me.

"How'd you know I came from Crile?" I began to slide off the stool, suddenly warm.

"Hell, the bag, the suit, the limp, the thousand-yard stare. I was in Percy Jones myself when I got back."

"Yeah, I guess it's easy. I guess you can tell."

"And I see you guys everytime I come through. Same bag, same suit, same limp, same stare. Not so many anymore."

"No, not so many anymore. Some day maybe none."

"You guys want another beer?" the woman spoke up.

"Yeah, Mae, one more and then I got to hit it." The man looked at me. "Another beer, kid? Some more of that piss?" He grinned.

I nodded and slid back on the stool. I resented his calling me "kid," but it was better than Mack or Joe or Sergeant or Sarge or the other nameless names that haunted what remained of my past. When Mae put the bottle in front of me I poured my glass full carefully, right to and bulging over the brim, then sat looking at it without thinking, making triangles with my thumb and forefinger again.

"You got wheels?" the man asked me then.

"Not in a long time." I hardly remembered the word.

"Which way you headed?"

"West."

"Where abouts?"

"Just West."

"I'm takin 82 to 20 at Elyria to 6 at Fremont and on into Indiana, if you want a lift."

"Sounds good." But they were just names, as empty as the shadows. I drained the glass and refilled it carefully. West was the direction you were supposed to take if there was nothing behind you; it was toward the setting sun, the part of American destiny. That was one thing I remembered. And another. When you went West in the other War, it meant you'd had it, you'd bought the farm, you had gone for broke once too often. Now it was the opposite of East. It was just a direction and nothing else.

"Let's shove." The man drained his glass, said "See you later, Mae," swung off the stool and walked to the door. I drained my glass, swung off my stool, and walked in his wake, and waved when he waved without turning as Mae said "Take it easy, fellas," and we were outside. The sun was brighter than before, and I squinted as I walked to the right side of the rig, pulled the door latch, tossed in my AWOL bag, swung into the left-hand seat. For a moment I saw GI brown on the hood, and then it was red, and I knew where I was. I rehearsed the route in my mind, and it too became real: 82 to US20 at Elyria and then across the Firelands of my past, the Lake to the North and the Western Reserve around me and the towns I once knew -- Elyria, Oberlin, Wakeman, Norwalk, Bellevue -- and what was once the Black Swamp and Big Turtle country and the Maumee, the river, and beyond, whatever there was beyond. I was suddenly alert and afraid and the driver thrust an open case of Iron City in the cab, positioned it on the gearbox between us and swung in.

"Ain't the kind of fuel we used in the Red Ball, kid. Then it was babes and cognac." He slammed the door turned the key, and then looked at me. The engine roared.

"You know the Red Ball, kid?" He slipped in the clutch, shifted, and then, as the rig began to move, double-clutched and shifted again with a loud accompanying "Hah!" We moved slowly out onto route 82, heading West, the sun bright through the bugs dead on the windshield.

"Yah, kid, that's the way we did it in the Red Ball." He pulled a bottle out of the case and opened it under the dash in one smooth movement. "That, too, kid." He handed me the bottle and opened another for himself. "All we need are the babes, huh?" He tilted the bottle and I did the same. It was warm, and I almost gagged. He laughed. "No coolers in the Red Ball, either, kid." He shifted again, and the rig behind us protested with a rattle. A car behind us honked, and he stuck protested with a rattle. A car behind us honked, and he stuck his arm out the window, fist clinched, middle finger extended. "Don't fuck with the Red Ball, man. Nobody fucks with the Red Ball."

He accelerated, and the rig groaned again. He tipped his bottle, drained it, and then stuck the empty back in the case. "Actually it wasn't all that great. The Red Ball. But we did move the stuff -- gas and ammo and rations -- when we could get in -- when they didn't want to slow old B&G up. Old Patton, that is."

He opened another bottle. I drained mine and took another, fumbled until I found the ridge under the dash for an opener. "We hauled for the Third Army exclusively. Across France, and then from the pipe heads and the rail heads." He pulled at his bottle, and kept talking about babes and bottles and all the things you could do at a steady forty-five. I made approving noises and every once in a while lit him a cigarette. He kept the rig at a steady forty-five and went on about the Red Ball and popped an occasional bottle.

He slowed to thirty-five and grinned at a parked patrol car as we passed through Eaton, founded 1818, and I remembered my great-grandparents buried there, dead nearly a century before I was born, part of a past I never knew and yet had lived with in the summers and had once nearly understood, and then suddenly I belched above the roar of the engine and the whistle of the wind.

He laughed loudly as he drained his bottle and tossed it at his feet. "Old Iron City tastes worse the second time around, kid. Cheap beer for cheap jags."

"Yeah," I said for the first time. "Like P.O.C."

"I was beginning to wonder, kid. Ain't sick, are you?"

"No. I'm not sick. Not anymore."

"You don't build up much resistance in places like Crile." He seemed suddenly subdued. "You were in there quite a while, weren't you, kid?"

"Yeah, Quite a while. Two years."

"Got hit bad, huh?"

"Yeah, pretty bad. But I'm okay now."

"Sure." He opened another beer. "Let me know when we get where you're goin." He took the cutoff onto route 57 into Elyria at his full forty-five, and the rig and cases and bottles shifted loudly. "You come from around here anyplace7"

I didn't know how to answer, so I said "Yeah. In a way," and then "I had relatives here a long time ago."

"Well, you let me know."

"Sure. They're all dead." I tried for a moment to remember: the Firelands and the farm in the summers and the Lake and the islands and the faces, all run together in my mind and in a sudden surge of warmth and I remembered what the shock treatments couldn't erase, the long lines of faces, of the dead, of all those that have a piece of me, but they wouldn't focus, and yet they wouldn't go away. I stuck my face out into the airflow and caught dust in my eyes. Once I had a notebook and a memory and now one was gone and the other faded, and I tried to remember.

"Yeah, the Red Ball was somethin."

"Sure was."

"You know anybody in it?"

"No."

"You get into France? Get some of that cognac?"

"No. I was in Italy."

"No Red Ball there, I bet."

"No. Lots of mountains. And mules."

"And babes, I hear."

"Yeah. Some." Suddenly I almost remembered. A face laughing, eyes flashing, almost a name.

"What you guys down there think about Normandy?"

Again, what could I say?" I didn't remember Normandy, except what some guys had said back in Crile. I must have been in the hospital on the hill in Naples. I didn't remember. I still can't remember.

"Great show," I told him.

"Yeah, great show. I wish I'd been in it."

"Something to tell your grandchildren."

"Yeah." He opened another bottle, held it between his knees, and cruised down Broad Street in Elyria, suddenly become Route 20. He made all the lights. I caught a glimpse of the courthouse, of the square, a sudden memory of the Victorian street where Sherwood Anderson, a name out of the past, had once lived. He made all the lights, and then we were headed West again, for the Firelands and beyond.

"Nice driving," I told him.

"Yeah. No, the Red Ball wasn't all that great."

"No. Nothing was."

"Nothin but pushin them six by sixes."

"A lot of driving."

"Yeah. And check points and M.P.s. And a sore ass. Hard on the kidneys, too.

"Yeah." He tossed an empty out the window, opened another, and drank.

"Piss call pretty soon."

"Yeah."

"And another case of Piss from Pittsburgh."

"Yeah." We passed south of Oberlin, where I remembered something, and it was lost quickly as we passed the county line into the Firelands that had been part of my collective past as the road ran along the great ridge that once, in pre-history, marked the lakeshore but now was lined with fruit trees showing traces of pink.

"Actually I hated the goddamn Red Ball."

"Sounded pretty good to me."

"Yeah. Garrison caps with a fifty-mission crush. And the big Red Ball on the door. And all the vehicles named: Dragon Lady. Miss Fitz. Der Fuhrer's Face, in a big brown turd. We were really somethin, I tell you." He laughed." The big Red Ball. The big Q.M." He finished the bottle and tossed it out. "We got to get rid of the evidence." He belched.

I tried to listen, and yet I didn't want to. He remembered better than he knew, better than I could, and yet I knew how it had been. Sooner or later, past or future or everlasting now you had to turn and face the dogs that tried to tear you apart, but the dogs had become shadows lost between the grease-smeared electrodes, and I began to shake, quickly took another beer, tried to look out, to see the Firelands around me, to see beyond the horizon to the lake beyond, tried to see where I was, where I had come from, but there was nothing but the shadow.

"You okay, kid?"

"Sure."

"We'll piss pretty soon. There's a roadside rest just out of Wakeman."

We passed through Wakeman at speed, where the New York Central runs along the main street, and I tried to remember, and then the rig slowed, pulled off to the side on a gravel shoulder, and stopped.

"Nothing fancy. The one-holer of your choice." He opened the door and swung down. I followed over to the shelter, the pump, the posted road map, went in one side suddenly conscious of a pressure in my gut, and then felt it ease as I hit the hole, and I knew that part of me had stayed in the hole. I buttoned up, ran into the sun, and climbed into the cab. I knew I should be feeling lightheaded, but I wasn't; I felt no-headed, and while I waited I opened another beer.

He opened his door, pushed another case across his seat, and then climbed in. "I smelled worse, but I don't know when. But when you gotta."

"Yeah."

"You okay, kid."

"Yeah. I'll get out pretty soon."

"Let me know." He started the rig, eased it onto the road in a horn blare, and laughed as the load groaned.

"Yeah, the fuckin Red Ball. An all the Piss of Pittsburg." He seemed suddenly to grip the wheel harder, almost bearing down on it. "Feels better goin out than in, sometimes. Damn trucks wreck your kidneys."

I finished my beer, and dropped the bottle at my feet, knowing that we were nearing Norwalk, that in many ways it was the beginning, that it should be the end, and I leaned back in the seat and closed my eyes. I could pretend to sleep; at least I didn't have to look, and the engine roared smoothly, the wind brushed my face; occasionally I heard an occasional muttered "fuckin Red Ball," and then I think I slept, but the faces were there, all those that owned me. And I owned a piece of each of them.

Somehow I had erased the past--that of the Firelands and of Norwalk and the innocence turned experience that it had become before the explosion and the screams and the shocks and the sudden, savage jolts of current that had presumably reordered my brain, or else I forgot, but when I opened my eyes a moment or an hour later the sun was lower in the sky and we heading directly into it

"Bout time, kid. We're on the long straight roll home."

"Where are we?"

"Route six west of Fremont. I cut off to miss the Toledo traffic."

Somehow I had missed the past--my own and my family's and the towns and the lake always there, and I felt almost fine.

"Have another beer, kid. Pretty soon we'll make another piss call." He pushed the accelerator, and the load rumbled behind us. He laughed and pushed it again. Suddenly he twisted the wheel, but it wasn't enough, and the load shifted again, and we paused for a moment and the world shattered in front of my face and the screams began—over the miles and the past, in my mind or not, and beer and blood and gasoline ran together in one pervasive smell each sharply etched and yet blended, and I knew that I saw and remembered and I knew that what I carried was in them and in me and it was death. When I awoke, the ward was quiet and I was in restraint, but I had no desire to move. I knew I had come back. Crile was home.

THE NIGHT I KILLED THE CAPTAIN

The clipping fell out of my mother's letter as I opened it,
alone in my book-lined room, and I knew immediately what
it was, knew the brief facts that it recited and the life that it
recorded and I was suddenly, deeply upset. It was Lenny's
obituary, and I knew what it didn't say: that he was loyal, fat,
a failure in the world's eyes and above all in his own;
instead, it said that he was dead at fifty-eight, officially of
lung cancer, that he was survived by a wife, that he would be
cremated without services. He had been a chain smoker since
he was fourteen, a habit we had acquired together, a habit I
had shed long before but he could not. But unofficially, I
knew sitting securely in my book-lined room, Lenny had
been dead much earlier, at the hands of people who failed
him and circumstances that destroyed him.

Most of my earliest memories are tied up with Lenny. He
was born on the Fourth of July, and there was a time when I
couldn't understand why his birthday was celebrated with
fireworks on hot summer evenings in the country and mine, a
month earlier, only with the usual cake and the ice cream that
we had taken turns churning. And I remember, too, Lenny
sitting blissfully in the back seat of a Model T Ford, chewing
industriously and rapidly on one candy orange slice after
another, and I remember the Christmas he was so pleased
with the fleet of toy cars "no bigger than my finger," and the
later Christmas, when, after the dirigible Akron sailed the
Ohio skies, each of us received its replica in heavy metal, big
and sturdy enough to ride on.

Lenny was a country kid and I was a city kid, but we were
tied together by a relationship neither of us fully understood

-- our mothers had been best friends since childhood, each the sister neither of them had, and we accepted without question the tie that bound them and us together. Winter holidays, especially Christmas, were spent with us in town, and much of each long, hot summer was spent on the farm in the heart of the Firelands, the vivid local history of which began, increasingly, to fascinate me, building my interest in place and time and people. And between holidays we exchanged occasional letters, studiously written, across the forty miles that separated us.

As we neared puberty in the mid-thirties, inevitably we grew separate identities. Although we still called ourselves the "Brain Trust" after FDR's controversial advisors -- I the "Brain," he the "Trust" -- already we knew that he, like the country out of which he came, was a Republican, I, like my small city on the lake, a Democrat. I became a Boy Scout, he, a bit later, a Lone Scout. I introduced him to the lake and the fishing boats tied up in the river and the men who sometimes promised that they would take us out to set the nets but never did; he took me to visit the five blond Carson girls down the road and to the town, two miles away, a gas station, a general store, and a bar in an old inn, once, fascinatingly, a station on the Underground Railway. But Lenny never learned to swim; I could never milk a cow.

But, city or country, we were fascinated by war. His father had been an infantryman, in the first war, then simply "the war;" mine had been an artilleryman, and we wore that heritage with a fierce pride, demanding stories from both, happily following their orders as they marched us down the lane or snapped us through a glorious close-order drill. In town I belonged to the "Ivory Patrol," patterned after that in the comic strip "Tim Tyler's Luck," and we fought

174

magnificent wars with kids from the next block; in the country we took turns wearing a battered helmet still emblazoned with the Big Red One of the First Infantry Division and lugged around an old Confederate musket that had belonged to my great grandfather, rebored as a shotgun and happily rumored to have blown a man's leg off when he was crawling through a fence hunting rabbits.

But times change; money became more readily available as the Depression eased, we discovered girls, with whom I enjoyed a modest, shy success. Lenny, as my town friends began to point out and I, reluctantly and with a curiously confused shame, was forced to admit, had become grotesquely fat, and he frustratingly was unsuccessful in love. I took Latin and science and read omnivorously, fascinated by words; Lenny took manual training and agriculture and later became a skilled carpenter and cabinet maker.

When the war broke out in Europe in September, 1939, however, we were fifteen, and we knew our destiny, afraid only that it would end before we were old enough to enlist. But we talked, on our increasingly rare meetings, of going to Canada across the lake. I was working in a Gulf station after school and on Saturdays for a tiny sad man whose glory had been our father's war, and Lenny had the chores, for which I had discovered a distaste. I went reluctantly to high school, my life spent on the basketball court, and with the newspaper accounts of the phony war, the strategy of the terrifyingly exciting days of 1940, and the German assault on Russia; Lenny went even more reluctantly to the consolidated school not far from the farm. Occasionally we shot baskets together, in the hoop on the end of the barn -- Lenny, in spite of what I thought was his incredible strength, could rarely hit the backboard -- and we talked about war.

In the fall of 1941 we were both seniors, and Pearl Harbor, that somber December Sunday, gave us both a sense of fearful joy; we had a rare telephone conversation, we extracted promises from our parents that they would "sign our papers" the day we graduated; we went through the routines that we hated; we enjoyed our destiny deliciously. And Lenny began desperately to diet.

But somehow I knew, and I know he knew, too, that he wouldn't make it, that his ankles, slightly injured playing football and aggravated by his great weight, would never pass, and I knew, and I think he knew, that his desperate diet couldn't last and couldn't possibly succeed. June came; I enlisted, we graduated, and at the family party we shared, Lenny said little as he furiously ate ice cream and cake. I was excited, I enjoyed the modest notoriety, and I left the next morning.

In the more than forty years since that party, I have seen Lenny perhaps half a dozen times, the first of them on what we thought was a wild, drunken night that was actually quite tame, just before I went overseas; again on a really drunken night in the spring of 1945; again at his wedding to a fat, friendly girl in 1949 at which I was best man; at a few circumspect family gatherings in the fifties, and then, the last deliberate, sad visit, with a deep sense of shame, just a month ago.

The war, fierce, intense, frightening, painful, much of it buried deep under psychological scar tissue, too much of it still vividly real, became and remains the central fact of my life and yet it is tied irretrievably to Lenny. He, farming, and working in a war plant, buying War Bonds, and writing occasional letters that I rarely answered, became the mythical 4-F that we joked about, taking the money, drinking the booze, screwing the girls that we would never know even though I knew it wasn't true; I, in the wet Tunisian winter, the bright Sicilian summer, formed the fierce, fast, quickly vanishing dependencies that passed for buddyship, drank prodigious quantities of bad wine and fraudulent cognac, screwed desperately in grimy rooms, became old at nineteen, and in a brief summer respite fell futility, fleetingly in love.

In Italy I was steady, dependable, an old timer, knowing the end that had eluded me was ahead, that I think I sought on the fragile beachhead at Salerno, in the mountains, in Yugoslavia, in the back streets of a typhus-ridden Naples, on what became *the* Beachhead at Anzio. The cool facts of a mutual survival, the obscenities of hate, the violent reality, the eternal wet, the next hills frustratingly on the horizon were what it was all about, were all any of us knew. And then came the night I killed the captain.

The First and Third Ranger Battalions had moved out through the wire, the mines, the end of January dusk, to take, like a piece of cake, the old market town of Cisterna that sat in ruins astride Highway 7, the old Appian Way that fed the enemy defense at Casino. We were in reserve, ready to move in, secure the town, do what we had landed to do a week before. We were, as always, nervous, uncertain, but somehow reasonably calm.

And then something -- intelligence, reconnaissance, command, but not will -- went horribly wrong, and we huddled in our holes, hearing the frantic communications, the fierce fire, knowing the hopelessness of dead friends, the tenuousness of our own fragile survival. When, near dawn, the last communication came, from a sergeant whose name and words I remember yet, I must have gone momentarily mad, but I know I was frigidly calm.

The Captain called me a fool, a stupid son of a bitch, but did not forbid it, and I gathered a squad, a medic, a radio operator, and took off through the grey dawn, the wire, and a profound quiet, to find out what had happened, to pick up what stragglers survived. Reluctantly, cursing himself quietly, the Captain came along.

We moved within sight of the town, we found two numb survivors and a voluble, terrified Italian civilian, we were shelled and mortared, and we scattered in a fire fight. The Captain, in capable control, regrouped six of us in a shell hole; we established radio contact with the company CP, and we settled down, to wait out the day in silent depression, the sense of final defeat breathing heavily with us in the hole.

Then, just before dusk, the Captain, restless, decided to check a hole fifty yards away for survivors. I called him a stupid son of a bitch, and we gave him what cover we could as he went through what had once been a vineyard. Then something -- a mortar, a Schmeisser, a grenade -- caught him, and the screaming began. We huddled in horror in our hole and the screaming went on.

There was nothing we could do and the screaming went on. I could see him flounder, caught in wire, bleeding, and the screaming went on. Finally it was dark and the screaming went on. I may have screamed myself; I know I did in my mind. And I knew what had to be done. I fired a flare; I figured coordinates, had the radioman call for the mortars; there were a series of thumps, and the screaming stopped. But then it began again, and I knew it was in my mind.

The rest of it I barely remember. There were two men in the other hole; they had heard the screams and the mortars; they joined us, and somehow we came back in the dark, each of us carrying the screams and the knowledge with us, some to our graves, those of us yet alive hearing and knowing in our dreams what we -- I -- cannot admit: that I killed the Captain, that I killed him because I was afraid, because I couldn't stand the screaming, his or that in my mind.

A few days later I was badly hit and evacuated, neither of which I remember, and the screams may have been my own. Then, amid the pain and the probing, in a brief ceremony in the hospital on the hill overlooking Naples they gave me the medal that for years I could not admit that I owned. Finally, with my war behind me, the pain and the probing gradually stopped, and the healing began.

In the spring of 1945, with the war in Europe winding down, I was pronounced healed, and I came home, not to the only but to the last place on earth that I wanted to be, utterly alone, lost, angry, empty, healed. And Lenny -- faithful, fat, friendly Lenny -- came to town to welcome me back, and we went out on the town.

It was a horrible night, of the kind I had come, perversely, in passes from the hospital, to enjoy, to drown what I could not forget. We drank in all the cheap bars that lined the main street of the town's south end; I knew, and I think Lenny knew, that I was looking for trouble. By ten o'clock I was cool, controlled, but I felt numb. And then it happened, and I'm deeply ashamed.

Lenny -- fat, foolish, faithful Lenny -- asked if I would do him a favor, and I airily agreed. He asked me then if I could get him a discharge button, that he would like to have one, and he grinned, knowing I understood.

Part of me did; I knew that this was the one thing we hadn't shared, the war that we both had wanted so desperately, that we could share its symbol if not its reality, that, at least in appearance, he could have what he missed, that somehow childish dreams would become something more. And yet, suddenly, I thought what could he know, and something within me snapped; foolishly, fiercely I began to hit him. I was screaming as the blood came from his mouth and he stood there, his bulk unmoving. Finally I stopped, and I began to cry in frustration, in shame, in humiliation. Lenny stood bleeding in silence.

During the decade that followed, our few meetings were oddly formal, my drunken excesses gradually easing as I finally found direction, purpose, love, success, perhaps even meaning, except in the dark hours, and Lenny, growing even fatter, became bitter, full of self-hate and hate of the world that despised him. Then, married to his fat schoolteacher wife, living in the old farmhouse, he became, by choice as well as his grotesqueness, a recluse. Finally, two months ago my mother wrote that he was dying of lung cancer, that he wanted to see me.

After nearly a month of indecision and shame I drove down. He was in the hospital in town, now no longer drab, and smelling of ether, but cheerful and new. He had lost much of the weight that he hated; what remained was pastily white; he talked in a violent whisper; he planned to be cremated, the ashes buried in a jar. And finally I left, knowing what I had done, what all of us had done.

The clipping was brief, factual, in its record of a life and a death. I put it back in the envelope, put the letter aside unread, dreading but resuming my life in the book-lined room.

A NOT SO CASUAL AFFAIR

Last night, as is often more likely than not, I couldn't sleep and thinking depressed me, and almost in desperation, as I do more frequently in recent years -- it's either that or the bottle, I joke, not without a measure of truth -- I turned on the *Tonight* show. It was a re-run of indeterminate age, but Carson was his inane self, and I began to yawn. Then the curtains beside him stirred and suddenly two generations of my life disappeared. I was young and in uniform and innocent, and it was the beginning of a long war, and I was more alive than ever before or since, and I remembered how it had been.

I liked New York in September of 1942. I had come there by Catalina flying boat from San Juan with stops in Miami and Charleston, but, too, like Fitzgerald's Nick Carroway a generation earlier I had come out of the West -- out of what had become clearly the Midwest by my time -- and in spite of the brownout I liked the racy, adventurous feel of the city at night. I walked Fifth Avenue and Park and sensed the excitement of men and machines and the slick women like those I had seen only in my mother's and sister's fashion magazines. Like Sherwood Anderson I tried to reach out in my mind to enter their lives, to know them, perhaps to be part of them, if only for a moment. But I didn't know how.

I knew that if it could be done, it would be only for a moment, not only because Sherwood Anderson had said so and because he had said that such moments were all that made human life possible, but because unlike Nick Carroway, who had come to New York to escape what was and perhaps to find what would be, my New York was a waystation, a

181

momentary break in the war that I was convinced would be for me as an earlier war had been for my father and for the new young writers who came of age in the decade of my birth the central experience of my generation. New York would become part of me, as would the days, months, perhaps years ahead of me.

At eighteen, not quite four months after my graduation from high school I was a demolition specialist, an expert rifleman, and a casual, detached from my unit and suspended in time. A bout of fever had kept me in Puerto Rico after my demolition section had completed its training and departed by transport for a rendezvous point at sea and an amphibious landing somewhere. I was the lucky one, to follow by air, special orders cut, a low priority assigned.

And so I flew to New York to follow and meet the ships and men that I later learned were moving South from Britain, and East from New York and Newport News. But my priority, like my rank, was low; my departure date was early November.

And so I reported in daily at 8:00 AM and I was free. I slept in a Times Square hotel and I read a great deal -- it was then that I discovered Thomas Wolfe, whose prose overwhelmed me with excitement. I imagined that I lived the life around me, moment by moment. And I began gradually to share it: the theaters at service men's rates, the museums, the music on 52nd Street, then Swing Street, the things one could do at eighteen and alive, in uniform in New York, in the fall of 1942.

At the end of my first week in New York I met Gloria. It was at a party in the West Eighties just off Central Park West, and I had come with a musician from the NBC symphony orchestra whom I had met in a bar, in Jack

Conway's, near Rockefeller Center. It was like no party I had ever known: it was movement, talk, glitter, color. I knew no one and my new friend had disappeared, so I drank scotch old-fashions, a measure of my new sophistication, returning as frequently as I dared to the bar in the dining room. I wandered the four crowded rooms, exchanging an occasional comment, catching snatches of conversation, first names that meant nothing, phrases that I stored as further material for my sophistication and my future literary career. There were two or three other uniforms.

Above the dim and smoke in a crowded hall I tried to strike up a conversation with a thin, dark haired girl with deep-set eyes who seemed alone. We exchanged names -- I recognized hers, the daughter of a famous composer, married to a well-known, notorious band leader. She began to bite her lower lip and seemed suddenly nervous. I offered to get her a drink; she seemed grateful; when I returned she was gone.

With two drinks in my hand I felt foolish alone, and, drinking, I slowly made my way, with apparent purpose, to the piano where a bald, red-faced man in a tuxedo was playing, unheard in the noise. He nodded, I nodded, put down one glass, nearly empty, sipped at the other, and pretended to listen. He played flashily but well, some show songs I knew and others I didn't. But mostly I watched. I got another drink, and returned to the piano, telling myself that this was New York, that it was real, that I was part of it. I knew I was slightly drunk and alone and I felt a bit foolish, but I liked it, I was excited by the noise, the smoke, the bits of music that I heard. I was looking for something, I knew, but I didn't know what.

Then, across the room, near the door, in a momentary rift in the crowd I saw why I had walked the streets of New

York, what I had wanted to reach out and touch, what I wanted to know. Nearly as tall as I, she had long, dark, wavy hair, green flashing eyes, a fine-boned face. She was perhaps twenty-two, but I liked older women. I thought she was alone, and our eyes met for a moment.

I put down my glass, began to make my way toward her, hoping as I lost sight of her that she was alone. But she wasn't; as I came near she was talking to a naval officer who seemed younger, newer than I. I stopped, watched them, uncertain what to do, came a bit closer. Her face was animated; his seemed flushed; I felt just as flushed and a bit nervous, even a bit futile. As I began to turn away, back toward my vantage point near the piano I caught another glimpse. She was alone and looked as ill at ease as I was beginning to feel. Not sure what I was doing, suddenly I was in front of her. Feeling even more foolish, I grinned.

"I hope you're enjoying the party."

She smiled. It was dazzling and she was younger than I thought. Her green eyes should have seemed incompatible with her face but weren't. "Are you the host? Or can I tell the truth?"

"I'm not. But I'm not sure what I am. And you should always tell the truth."

That smile again. "Are you trying to crowd a lot of living into a three-day pass, too?"

I grinned back. "No, I've got five more weeks."

"Practically a lifetime."

"I thought it was. Now I'm not so sure. It may be several."

"Nobody has several. But it would be nice."

"Yes, it would." I paused. "Can I get you a drink?"

184

"No, thank you. I'm not going to stay."

"But I thought . . ."

"That I came with someone? I did. But his lifetime is only three days."

"That's not very long."

"It could be too long." She wrinkled her nose. "Besides, I know him too well."

"Oh?" I didn't know what else to say.

"I knew him at the studio. Before he joined the navy."

"The studio?"

"NBC. I'm a page."

"Oh. You live in New York." It was a statement, but I knew. I glanced down. She was wearing a black sweater, black pleated shirt, high heels.

Unlike the women on Fifth Avenue, she didn't glitter. She shone.

"What do you do?"

I grinned. "Can't you tell?"

"I mean before."

"I was in school."

"College?" "No."

"Oh. I'm in high school, too. This is my last year."

"But you work."

"Only from six to ten, three nights a week."

I wasn't sure what to say. When I was a senior -- a year ago -- I was still delivering the *Plain Dealer* before school. She seemed to sense my discomfort:

"It's good experience for me, although my mother doesn't like it. I go to the High School of Performing Arts." I could almost hear the capital letters.

That was the beginning. It was innocuous and innocent enough, as it was to remain, and in retrospect it sounds flat. But it was a good deal more, and I think we both knew it at the time. The young naval officer -- Jack, I think she called him -- with the untarnished gold braid on his cap had disappeared in the smoke and the talk and I never saw him again. After a few more minutes of talk that seemed to me -- and I think to her, too -- to go beyond time-filling chatter, she looked up at me. Her green eyes were magnificent.

"I've got to go. It's been a long day."

"For a seventeen-year-old." I wanted her to stay. Unlike the women of Fifth Avenue, she was real. For a moment I was back in Ohio. "Can I walk you home?"

She laughed. Her green eyes laughed too. "Sure. Its only ten blocks." She lived on 77th near West End, and that walk was the beginning of a good deal of walking that we were to do in the five weeks that remained. On the way she told me a good deal about herself, her family, her plans, her ambitions, especially her ambitions. None of my contemporaries knew what they wanted to do, but she was clear: she would be an actress, preferably legitimate, but unlike her schoolmates she refused to sneer at Hollywood. She had an agent. She had some talent, but not enough, she was afraid. Her father was a pianist in theater orchestras, her mother a photographer's assistant with ambitions for herself and for Gloria. Her parents were separated. Her father -- a tall, silent, shadow-like man whom I was later to see at odd intervals -- was Jewish, her mother, a tiny, intense woman whom I was to see almost daily, was Irish. "I hate the combination -- it frightens me, and sometimes I think it makes me nothing, or nothing clear. And sometimes I hate them." She, like her mother -- her parents were married outside the Church, but she didn't believe in divorce -- was nominally Catholic. She enjoyed High Mass, but her mother rarely went. All the time she was holding my arm and looking up at me under the street lamps. Even in the shadow I could see the green of her eyes.

I didn't say much; there seemed very little about myself worth saying. The brisk, clear voice, the laugh, somewhat high but clear, I liked; the somewhat self-deprecatory tone I didn't. I knew that she was better than she knew, but I didn't know how to tell her so. And perhaps I was afraid to tell her. Even at eighteen I knew there was something magical about Gloria. Nearly half a century later there is still a magic about her, a magic that no popular medium can suppress or distort.

As we walked west on 77th Street we were hand-in-hand, swinging our arms and laughing. I didn't know what I was saying -- whatever popped into my head, much of it the sincerest possible flattery of which an eighteen-year-old is capable, and she giggled, protesting, liking it. When we arrived at the four-story brownstone carved into flats -- a week later I rented a top-floor one-room "efficiency" for the remaining four weeks -- Gloria rang the bell. When a voice, precise but flat, said "Yes," she said "Mom, I'm home," the buzzer rang, she squeezed my hand and rang again. "In a minute, Mom,"

"All rght." This time the voice sounded tired.

I reached out, she came against me, and I held her as tight as I could. Her slimness seemed intensified; she seemed to melt into me and I kissed her. Neither of us knew how to open our mouths until we learned intuitively. "French

187

kissing" was talked about, giggled about among my peers of both sexes, but "nice" girls kept their lips tightly closed -- but it came easily.

"Careful," she gasped in a moment. "I may be the only seventeen-year-old virgin in New York."

The word excited me, and I kissed her again. The buzzer sounded again, and she moved away gently, smiling in the dim light. "My mother's impatient -- or tired -- or afraid -- for me." Her laugh was musical but a bit shrill. "I've got to go up." She laughed again. "In a minute."

For a moment I didn't know what to say, and I was suddenly terrified that I wouldn't see her again.

"You could come up. But the apartment's quite small, and I'm sure mother's not dressed."

I heard myself saying "It doesn't matter," and I had no idea what she meant, but she reached out and took my hand.

"Of course not. But she thinks I'm out with Jack, and you don't look a bit like him." She giggled, wrinkling up her nose, and pushed the button. I held back. "Will she be upset?" I had visions of an irate mother ordering me out the door.

"Of course not." The door buzzed again, and she opened it.

I held back. "When will see I you again?"

She laughed again. "Whenever you want."

"Tomorrow?"

"Sure. It's Saturday. But I work in the evening, from six to ten."

"And I have to report in at 8:00 in the morning."

"I'll be still asleep." She pulled me in the door and to a tiny elevator, opened it.

"It's hard to be formal in a place like this," she laughed and leaned up against me. The momentary terror was gone and so was the fear of embarrassment. We rode up slowly, not staring at the numbers, as people do when thrown into such close proximity in elevators. We looked at each other. The door opposite was ajar.

"Mom, I'm really home. And I have someone with me."

"Jack?"

"No. Someone nicer. Can we come in?"

I had always hated to meet girl's parents because, although my intentions were always honorable -- or at least not dishonorable -- I was reasonably sure they would think otherwise. And yet -- I may be flattering myself -- girls' parents always liked me. I was so polite. And in spite of the amount I had drunk I felt sober. But I was high with what I was convinced was love.

Mrs. Bernard, in her robe, with her hair up and carefully covered, seemed to think I was all right. After an initial rather stiff introduction -- although Gloria was delightful, even when she couldn't quite remember my last name -- it became evident that Gloria was the center of her existence, that her natural suspicion of and curiosity about a strange male in uniform coming in at midnight with her daughter was tempered by her trust in Gloria's judgment. It was evident, too, that she seemed relieved that -- as she later commented -- I was well beyond the "dese and dose" stage that seemed to represent the educational achievement of most of the enlisted men and non-commissioned officers she had met. She made coffee, we talked for half an hour about me, about where I was from and where I was reasonably sure I was going. But most of her talk, to which Gloria agreed with occasional comments, was where her daughter was going. I interpreted her comments as maternal pride and ambition tempered by a mild warning. Nevertheless, I liked her, I felt at ease with her, and I sensed that like so many others I had met in New York that Fall, she was genuinely concerned about whatever it was that was ahead of me.

It was that time of the war when whatever optimism any of us had was tempered by the news. Guadalcanal was a bloody stalemate, and the offensive in Europe seemed remote, either on the Eastern front or in the anticipated landings in the West. But in Puerto Rico we had assaulted the simulated defenses at Mers-el-Kebir in Algeria, and I felt confident, telling them that the war and the news would turn soon. I felt adult, assured, I suppose, a man.

I knew I should leave but I wasn't sure how, and I was afraid to. My high had dissipated in talk that was essentially serious -- about Gloria's future that was strangely but clearly if unspokenly contrasted with my own -- and my masculine confidence was shattered in the process. Finally, as the conversation flagged, I did what I knew I should do -- the inevitable control over my own behavior, I later learned. I rose, thanked Mrs. Bernard for her hospitality, and said that I must be going. And silently I pleaded with Gloria to walk me to the elevator. The earlier moments seemed unreal, and I needed reassurance badly. She rose with me. With a sudden surge of joy, I felt suddenly nervous as I shook hands with her mother and exchanged goodnights. I was so Goddamned formal and stiff, but I couldn't help it.

"I'd better let you out downstairs. The nightlock is tricky." It was more than I hoped for, but I replied formally that she needn't, she insisted, and Mrs. Bernard agreed. In a moment we were in the elevator, close but apart, both of us silent. Finally, as it strained to a stop, I spoke.

"I do want to see you tomorrow. But I'm not sure that I should."

"Don't let Mother frighten you off. She's afraid I'll run off and get married or something."

"You're much too young for that," I said as we stepped into the narrow hall.

"It isn't that. I'm Mother's justification."

"Justification?"

"Yes. She thinks I'm more talented than I am. But mostly for marrying my father -- and for leaving him, too."

"I think your mother is right."

"About marriages? Or me? Or my father?" She was laughing at me, but it was contagious, and I laughed, too.

"I don't want to contribute to your mother's fears."

"I think she likes you, so don't be afraid."

"But I should go."

"I think she trusts you, too."

I grinned. "I trust me. And most mothers do."

"Irish mothers?"

"My mother is Irish -- half Irish -- and she trusts me."

"Mine is all Irish, and I don't think there's a man in the world whom she trusts. But I can tell she likes you."

"If I hang around much longer, she won't."

"But she trusts me. God knows she's told me enough about men."

"Do you believe it?"

"Of course not. And yet part of me does."

"Which part?"

"I don't know. Maybe the Irish in me. Or maybe the Jewish." She was serious for a moment, and then she looked up at me, her eyes wide and shining. I kissed her gently for what seemed a long time, and she kept her eyes open, watching me. Then she drew away. "Now go. But come tomorrow. At noon."

Outside I looked at the brownstone for a long moment, impressing it on my mind, and then, through a soft rain, I walked back to the hotel, whistling in the rain for nearly thirty blocks. And then I read *Look Homeward Angel* until dawn.

Saturday marked the beginning of a relationship that lasted until my travel orders were cut, and in a way it continues yet. At eight I reported in; at twenty after, I was on the street, savoring the city that was suddenly no longer a spectacle. It was a beautiful day, with a hint of Fall in the air when at noon exactly I climbed the steps of the brownstone on 77th Street. Gloria was waiting just inside the door. We walked over to 81st and Broadway, debated a moment what to do, and then rented bicycles. We rode through the park, out and around Grant's Tomb, and back through the park, always within talking distance, almost within touching distance, even when I showed off: steering with my feet, standing on the seat, cutting close and touching her uncertain hand.

Finally she pulled over to a grassy slope, dropped the bicycle on its side, and stretched out. I fell beside her, and we both breathed hard for a moment.

"I haven't done this in years. I'm all out of breath."

"I haven't either." That wasn't quite true. It was just over a year.

"I like being with you."

"Me, too."

We were both silent for a minute. I rolled over on my side to watch her. She was on her back, looking up at the trees." I like to look at you," I finally said.

"I like to have you look at me." She turned to face me. "And I like to look at you. I thought about you a lot last night."

"And I thought about you."

"Five weeks isn't very long."

"No." But it seemed a lifetime at the moment.

"There's a lot to talk about."

"We've got lots of time."

"Not that much. And I've got to go to work."

We got back on the bicycles, returned them at 81st Street, and walked over to 77th and West End. She changed while I sat on the stoop, we walked over to the Automat on Broadway, had sandwiches and coffee, and then, neither of us talking, I held her close in the vestibule of the subway car down to 51st Street. We walked slowly over to the NBC Building, and I stood watching as she walked confidently into the building, head-high, hair flying, arm-swinging, the public Gloria, smiling privately. She knew I'd be waiting at ten.

That first Saturday set the pattern for the five weeks that followed. My life revolved around her schedule, and I found myself counting the minutes and hours since I saw her and until I would see her again. That night, while waiting, I didn't go to a bar. Instead, I walked to the North River and for a long time stood watching the Weehawken ferry as it lost itself in the gloom of the Jersey shore and then re-emerged, back and forth, and I thought about Gloria -- or more properly, she filled my mind. I hardly heard the noise from the expressway overhead. I didn't need -- or want -- people or lights or glitter or chatter or the not-yet-started *Of Time and the River* in my room. At ten I was waiting. We had coffee and then took an old Fifth Avenue bus uptown, sitting upstairs alone, necking gently, and then walked slowly across the park. Mrs. Bernard was waiting up.

In a week, by the time I moved into the top floor one-room flat, the pattern had become fixed, varied only by Gloria's schedule, and the five weeks became four and three and two and one and then none. They passed in vignette, each of them sharp even yet. Together they made up thirty-five days of my life and Gloria's, days that marked the end rather than the beginning of something, although then both of us were convinced that they were a beginning. And what had begun as a crush, a late adolescent attraction, had, we believed, become a great deal more, had become permanent.

We did the things that we did in the beginning: we walked, we necked in busses, subways, and hallways; each day I met her after school, and on working days we ate in the Automat, and I waited. On Sundays we had a late breakfast with her mother, and then Gloria and I went to 1:00 PM Mass across the park. We lunched on hot dogs at the zoo, and we walked. We went to plays at service men's rates—for dates too -- and to a great many movies -- Gloria loved them, insisting that she was studying them, and I tolerated them for her, sometimes distracted her with my love, sometimes pretended to doze, and sometimes did. Once, when her mother was out, she insisted that my fingernails were too long for a man, and she cut them shorter than I liked. I submitted meekly, happily. And then she pretended to read my palm, predicting long life, great success, much love.

I remember, too, the private Gloria, her face tender, close, love-filled, her green eyes shining, in those moments, many of them, when we held each other tightly, even more tightly as the five weeks passed, each day more quickly than the day before. But she didn't come to my room -- until the last night -- nor I to hers. We weren't afraid; we were sure.

But most of all we learned that we could talk -- about ourselves and to each other. I learned about the stormy balance she tried to maintain between her two identities, between her father and her mother, her Jewishness and her Irish Catholicism, between two demanding cultures and people. She loved both and she hated both, often at the same time. She remembered a Christmas when she was quite young: shouts, tears, blows struck, and she didn't know why.

I learned, too, about her ambition, her determination to succeed as an actress, her eagerness to work, to construct a public Gloria, an identity apart from the confused self-image that had distorted her life. She was a mongrel, she insisted, but she would become a thoroughbred. The Gloria that the public would know -- and that she was convinced, she would know, would be apart from her mother's guilt-ridden Irish Catholicism and her father's cultural Jewishness. She might -- she was uncertain -- maintain some sentimental or aesthetic ties with either or both -- but she would be an actress, and a good one. Her determination, her willingness to work, her mother's ambition for her -- for all the wrong reasons -- would make up for whatever she lacked in talent. And

Each time she talked about the future -- her future -- her voice was clear and low, with a curiously cold passion.

Without such determination -- my future, at least for a while, was less clear -- I had no particular ambitions except a vague knowledge that someday I would write. I argued -- mildly but with conviction. A public image -- and acting -- had nothing to do with identity. That had to do with what was inside. And she could not create it, she had to find it and free it. I knew her, I insisted, and I liked her, but she had to know herself, too.

My arguments, like her ambition, were typically adolescent, and she could not or would not understand. And I wasn't as convincing to myself as I tried to sound. I knew that I had a public identity—the uniform I wore, the orders I was under, and the oath I had taken -- and too often I was afraid I was becoming something other than I was. I didn't like what I was -- I felt as confused and dissatisfied about myself as she did - nor did I like what I was afraid I was becoming.

And I didn't like to talk about it but I did. I told her about one incident that had haunted me for years—since the final grade. I too was a mongrel. My Ohio town, a steel town, was a confused mass of nationalities -- Polish, Russian, Italian, and a variety of Slavs, and real Americans -- descendants of English, Irish, and German ancestors who had arrived there before the mills, who had merged and intermarried and who, whether Catholic or Protestant, kept aloof from the newcomers and kept careful control of the town. Their identity as Americans, forged in the Civil War, was clear. And, I knew intuitively before I was six that I was one of them.

And, I knew intuitively before I was six that I was one of them.

My first grade class at Harrison School reflected the makeup of the town, and before the first week I was torn between two loves, dark-haired, brown eyed Norma Niccoletti and blue-eyed, blond-haired Maxine Mauer. But of course, I was terrified of speaking to either. Early in those first months my teacher asked several of us -- carefully selected, I suspect -- what nationalities we were. One -- Norma -- was Italian, others were a Pole, a Slovenian, even a Macedonian. But I didn't know what I was.

That afternoon I asked my mother, and an uncle who was visiting told me to tell the teacher that I was a "Yankee mongrel." The next day, very seriously, I did. She giggled, and after a moment, said, "That's nice." I didn't understand the giggle, but I never forgot the incident, and even after I understood -- a year or two later -- I didn't think it was funny. Nor did Gloria as I told her about it.

Like her I was a hybrid, a mixture, with competing identities, mild puritan, Waspishness on my father's side, strong puritan Irish Catholicism on half of my mother's. From my father I learned duty, honor, responsibility, country, from my mother I absorbed a burden of guilt, and I resented both. I resented, too, the strain of Irish wildness, of latent -- and sometimes overt -- violence, somewhat tempered by a gentle humor, that I saw in my uncles and sensed in myself. The strains reinforced each other, and I tried to reject both, but neither Puritanism nor my guilt would leave me alone.

To Gloria it was simple and clear; like her I had to forge my own identity, one that I could accept, and live with. I knew it was clear but I knew too that it was not simple. I had to understand and direct what I was, what was in me. And I knew she had to do the same, but I wasn't sure either of us could. But our knowledge if not understanding of each other brought us closer, and she began to talk more frequently of an after-the-war future together. I would write; she would star; and we would rise above whatever was tearing both of us apart.

Her enthusiasm was confident and almost contagious, but I was conscious of time, the war, and myself in a way that she could not be. And I was aware, too, that neither the war nor my own nature could permit me to share in her faith in the future -- any future, particularly for me. I'm sure she sensed that something inside me was holding back, but that was one thing we didn't discuss.

Suddenly the six weeks were over. On the morning that the paper had carried the first reports of Allied landings in Morocco and Algeria, I knew what I had missed, but I knew, too, where I was going. I reported in at eight; my orders were cut. When I met her after school, neither of us had much to say. Our routine was outwardly much like those of the days and weeks before: it was a crisp, clear November day, and we walked, hand-in-hand from 53rd Street to 71st street; we ate in the Automat -- "Good food and quite inexpensive" she joked, parroting her mother, as she had the first time. We walked and sat in the park. She called her mother to tell her she wouldn't be home until late and I said goodby to her briefly, inanely, by phone, acknowledging her good wishes and advice. Without discussion we went cautiously to my room two floors above her mother and we lay on the bed all night fully dressed, holding each other tightly, knowing that we were trying to preserve a contact that was rapidly slipping away. At four I gathered my gear and slipped away quietly, leaving Gloria asleep on the bed. I reported in at the Air

Transport Section of the Port of Embarkation at 6:00, and at noon I was in the air in a C54, New York lost in the haze somewhere behind me.

I saw Gloria again in the late spring of 1945. I was on convalescent leave; she had just closed as the second lead in a Broadway show and had auditioned for another. We had written -- she almost daily at first and I less frequently -- and in the dark, cold days after Kasserine Pass while waiting for replacements at Constantine I had received a tattered copy of *Redbook* with her picture, intense and innocent, on the cover. But our correspondence dwindled, and sometime in late 1943 or early 1944 it stopped.

As the war was winding down, we met for lunch in Midtown, and at 20 she was well, prosperous, lovely, excited; at 21, I was old. We talked about her career, her few successes, her problems, her hopes, her continued ambition and confidence. I had little to say. How could I tell her about Tunisia, about Marinette who died, about the whores and the kids of Italy, the cold fear, the long month after I awoke in the general hospital in Naples and could not see, the Silver Star I had earned by getting seven men killed, the new guilt piled on the old. It was a long lunch, and we parted friends. We kept in occasional touch for a while, and that, too died; over the years I've seen her name and picture in the papers, and occasionally on the screen. When one of my books came out she wrote a brief note. And there she was at midnight, on the Johnny Carson rerun, laughing, green eyes flashing.

As she talked about her career, her hopes, her successes, her ambitions, I could sense the years evaporating; she looked and sounded great. She may even be happy.

HOME COUNTRY

He had driven almost aimlessly for nearly an hour over the narrow back roads -- Russell, Orphanage, Gore, Every -- quietly cursing the abrupt turns that mark the survey errors where the Western Reserve becomes the Firelands. He was driving through nearly two hundred years of his family and his genetic heritage while his mind refused to leave the complexities of his present of two days -- thirty-eight hours -- ago and six hundred miles East and the manuscript that tried to make sense of his life. His driving was no more aimless than the nearly quarter-millennium of the Ohio past that his errand would momentarily bridge, yet it seemed as purposeless as the too warm, too wet, too green day that was this first day of winter. He would complete his errand in an hour in spite of the perennial ache in his shoulder, he would erase the face of the present that tore at him from his mind and his life, and in a few days he would return to another past, the past of 1943, that lived in the reality of the pages of that manuscript that might ultimately give form and meaning to the three weeks of that Spring in Tunisia, nearly a half century ago. And then he would go on through the motions that had marked his life for more years of detachment than anyone needed or deserved.

The directions he had received from his mother at breakfast nearly two hours ago seemed clear enough, and he had been over those same roads many times in his own pre-war past, that of his childhood and adolescence, but his mother was nearly ninety and it had been more than a half century since he had known those back roads in the Firelands, and there had been many roads and paths and love and fear and violent pain and sudden death and a long, deliberate detachment since he had wandered them. But the errand was simple, and in the trunk was a shovel, an ax, and a bucket of gravel. He would find the graveyard, cut up and remove the tree that had fallen across the graves; straighten the stone, fill in under it with gravel and be gone. In an hour he would have completed the chore, rejected the face of the past become present that threatened him, and then, in a few days return to the manuscript that made the now remote past more real than he could ever let the present or the near past or the future become.

Finally, just over a rise that was called a hill in Northern Ohio he saw the tall, ragged pines that had come West from Connecticut as seedlings more than a century and a half ago and still brooded over the faceless, often nameless dead who had brought them. The cemetery was smaller than he remembered, and he saw that brush had intruded from the fence rows on three sides as he pulled over, straddling the grassy ditch in front of the gate. It could have been any of the dozens -- perhaps hundreds -- of the tiny mid-nineteenth century family graveyards scattered through the fields and brush and woodlots of the Western Reserve -- Firelands juncture, but he knew that it was the right one. But there was nothing familiar about it except the familiarity of the past, and he wasn't sure which of the thirty or more graves, stones atilt, mounds littered, was the right one. But it was there, he would quickly -- or slowly, his shoulder reminded him -- perform the chores that were perhaps the last that he would do for his mother and her past and the more remote one before it, and then he would be gone to a past and a reality of his own.

He sat for a moment staring through the rain-speckled windshield and then opened the door. A refrain echoed in his mind: let the dead past bury its dead. But the living must remember the graves, he added aloud, paraphrasing his mother and his grandmother. Overhead, between the leafless branches that met over the road, he saw a lone gull soar high, and motionless, twenty miles inland from Lake Erie, and then he watched it turn south along the ridge that sent its runoff impartially to the Ohio River and the lake.

He lit a cigarette and then got out of the car. It was raining more persistently than he realized, and the khakis, cotton jacket, and loafers were less than adequate, but he would find the graves -- near the center, he vaguely recalled -- get the tools, perform the job quickly and probably inadequately and be off. There was much more to be done, his mother had insisted; the cemetery's title had passed to the township years before, but it was badly maintained, although the sheriff had caught some teenage vandals a year or so before and made them clean brush and reset the stones -- those that weren't broken and laid flat -- that they had upset. But the vandals had, deliberately or not, contributed to the sense of identity lost that his mother complained about bitterly.

As he entered the gate, noting that the graveyard must have been grazed that summer -- a scratching cow had perhaps set his great-great grandparent's stone atilt -- he remembered that it had been laid out on Gilmore land in 1819 and the first long-lost, nameless grave had been dug shortly after his great-great grandfather had arrived from Connecticut, the warrant for eighty acres of Firelands land as payment for the farm land in Connecticut lost to a British raiding party, in his pocket. And the last grave -- that for his great-great grandmother -- had been dug in 1900.

He glanced at the fallow cornfield to his left, where his great-great grandfather had built the Congregational chapel the year after he had laid out the graveyard. He remembered the mounds that had marked the foundations when he was a boy, but they had disappeared, as had those of the old house, plowed into flatness a long time before; even the ashes that marked the old chapel's passing were obliterated as surely and finally as the family's Congregationalism, lost to a frontier Baptist revivalist and then, inexplicably, to the Catholicism of the quiet, introspective Irishman his grandmother had married, whose legacies were the reinforced Puritanism of his grandmother, his mother, and himself, and a movement to town and a temporarily revived family fortune.

The plot was also smaller than he remembered. The Gilmores were a durable but not a prolific people, he reflected, and he was the last of the line. It had reached its apogee when Cousin Quincy -- Major General Quincy Adams Gilmore -- had fired the Swamp Angel on Confederate held Fort Sumter and then had completed the circle when he went on to plant his seed and eventually his bones in the East out of which the family had come and he, himself, had gone East to stay, he reflected.

He wandered among the stones, stepping on his cigarette in a mass of wet pine needles, and tried to decipher the inscriptions -- a name, Sarah, wife of Samuel, a date, 1847, a barely-discernible weeping willow, a single finger pointed skyward. The last of the line, he thought again; the past makes us what we are and eventually it is merged with the present -- and we, it, both -- disappear. He was over sixty years old; he was reserved; he was staid; he was a Doctor of Philosophy; the past was his profession -- he interpreted two thousand years of human civilization for a faceless mass --

and the past had become his shield as well as his curse. Like his mother, he was not entirely comfortable in an age that seemed to have vulgarized and popularized sin, and the past was as much a protective device from that as it was a profession and a way of life. But it was also a burden, a ghost that the manuscript would exorcise -- or resurrect.

Then he saw it, the stone clear, but leaning dangerously forward. He took his handkerchief out of his pocket, rubbed the mist from his glasses and leaned forward to read through the jagged splinters of the lightening-struck pine between him and the stone. The outline of the weeping willow was dim as the soft sandstone eroded to earth, but the letters -- recut in 1900 -- were clear: John W. Gilmore -- Connecticut, July 1, 1795 -- Ohio, September 5, 1855 -- and then, Emily, his wife -- Connecticut, April 1, 1797 -- Ohio, May 15, 1900. Then, below, Gone to the Father -- Remembered by Their Sons. But there were no sons, he thought except the nameless infant and the lone cavalry corporal and Uncle Quincy, dust in a Victorian New York cemetery. There were daughters -- his great grandmother, his grandmother, but they were -- or would be -- buried elsewhere and there was himself. But he was not -- and yet he was -- a Gilmore. And he was faced with a chore that would be harder than he anticipated before he went back to the house on the lake and then in a few days drove six hundred miles East to the present and to his own past, nearly three hundred pages long.

He turned away to return to the car for the tools and the gravel -- and a bottle of brandy in the glove compartment. He lit another cigarette, paused to decipher other stones, almost all of them Gilmores, all of them old, all of them fading into earth. He had spent much of his life in cemeteries, he thought, and he felt curiously at home in them, even on those occasions when he stopped along some remote road to browse and to wonder. Much of his youth had been spent in this one -- with his grandmother and his mother, he playing while they weeded and remembered, and in the cemetery in town where his great grandmother, whom he dimly remembered as a tiny, white-haired lady in black, had been buried at 97 in 1929, beside the great grandfather who was a legend. And then in the Catholic cemetery across the road where lay the wild-eyed Irish grandfather who had given his grandmother her Catholicism, and revitalized her Puritanism, and two sons who died quickly; only his mother and he himself endured; the Irishman who lay there had invented an ore and coal unloading gadget still used on the lakes, and had left them their modest substance and the old house on the lake, together with their revitalized Puritanism. His grandmother was beside him now. She had been there since 1942, just before he went overseas at 18, and his father was there, too, buried while he was gone, and beside him was a place for his mother, the date on the stone yet in the future. There was room for him too, but he had no right to be there, nor would he ever be there again.

He reached the car feeling an intensified ache in his shoulder as he flicked the cigarette into the road and then opened the trunk and took out the axe and the shovel. Somewhere in the distance a shotgun boomed and echoed and he walked back to the graves, remembering other cemeteries -- at Mateur in Tunisia and at Nettuno, and the makeshift graves along the Italian roads he had walked countless times, where he should have been but had been cheated. And then suddenly he remembered the treeless cemetery on the hillside outside Tunis, with its weeping women in black, where they had buried all that they found of Marinette on an early summer day in 1943.

He stumbled, swore, and then put the tools down against the shattered trunk and returned to the car. Like many in the plot he had loved a woman and fought a war. But she had died and he failed to and he had been drunk for a long while as he tried to put it all on paper, and then he burned the paper and then he withdrew and went through the motions and they said he had readjusted well when he became a Doctor of Philosophy fifteen years after the war. He muttered shit, not knowing why, as he pulled the bucket of gravel out of the trunk. Then he remembered again the nearly three hundred pages of his past.

He carried the bucket -- at least forty pounds of gravel - quickly back to the grave, changing hands and stumbling as the ache in his shoulder became pain. He put it down in front of the stone and then remembered the brandy. He lit a cigarette and then returned for it. The damp air, he noticed, had become chilly. He flicked the cigarette, wiped his glasses again, and then opened the door and took the brandy out of the glove compartment. With the past nagging behind his eyes he walked quickly back to the grave, opened the bottle, and stared at the stone that was all that remained of his teetotaling, Congregational great-great grandparents, and he drank to them and the past. Then he put the bottle down carefully on the slanted stone and picked up the axe.

As he swung, slowly and steadily biting into the dry, shattered pine, he remembered the not-yet-two-days ago present, the past had become the pages of the present that alternately frightened and fascinated him in the dull normal world six hundred miles East. He chopped steadily, sweating a bit as he swung and the pain persisted. And the pages of other presents became the face of the past, the eyes the green that had matched the dress he had first noticed nearly half a century before.

At eighteen he had come of age in Central Tunisia, in the long nights after the rout at Kassarine Pass, and before he was nineteen he had come from the short, fierce fire-fight on Hill 609 to the sea at LaMarsa. He saw her standing on the walk at the edge of the beach, her face lighted by the green light reflected from the bay. Boldly he walked over and in his Army French and her schoolroom English they began to talk.

It was all in the manuscript and more, and it had been in the pages he had written and destroyed in the dead years after the war. He swung furiously, the chips flew, and the dry wood shattered. He paused, put down the axe, picked up the bottle and drank again. His shoulder paining, he put the bottle down. He walked over to the fencerow and urinated where he had more than half a century before. On his way back he paused at a squat partly sunken War Department issue stone and read: Ohio -- John A. Gilmore -- corporal, Fifth Ohio Cavalry -- 1845-1865. His great grandmother's younger brother, dead at twenty at Five Forks as his war was coming to its end. They had brought him home to be with his father as they would have brought him, and he would lie not at Mateur or Nettuno or Florence, but at his father's feet in the Catholic cemetery in town. And perhaps in Virginia, Corporal Gilmore had left a girl -- a woman -- even a grave, as he had on that hillside outside Tunis.

He picked up the axe again and chopped steadily and hard. The trunk snapped and snapped again, and in a few minutes it would be manageable; he could pull the pieces over to the fencerow. The brandy and the exercise warmed him comfortably, and the pain in his shoulder seemed to subside. The trunk shattered again, and it was enough. He put down

208

the axe and drank again. He felt a little guilty as he pulled the pieces one by one to the fencerow. Returning, he scattered the chips with his foot, burying them under the wet needles.

Taking the bottle, he returned to the fencerow, sat down on the trunk he had just dragged over, and drank again. Then he threw the bottle, still almost half full, into the brush. It landed near a bright aluminum beer can, the residue of a generation that he taught and that frightened and fascinated him, the generation of the faces that only rarely emerged from the mass of the present. He wiped his glasses again, lit a cigarette, and remembered.

It had been a brief three weeks by the sea, and it was innocent. They were both very young, and alive, and they walked by the sea and they played cards in the evening by lamplight, and occasionally they touched. She was seventeen and French and he felt old and American and she was unlike any girl he had ever known. Her mother was dead; her father, a major in the debacle of 1940, had brought her to Tunisia to live anonymously and safely by the sea. And then the three weeks were over, and she whispered I love you forever and he had gone to Sicily and in six weeks the letter had come.

It was in French -- her father knew no English -- but he knew what it said before he puzzled it out: the FW 190, damaged, out of control, had come over the town, and had jettisoned its bombs over the Place de France before disappearing into the bay. She had been home alone. They buried her in Tunis. Months later he had gone there and stood with her father beside the yet unmarked grave and then he had gone on to Italy and battles and bars and brothels and a decoration instead of oblivion, and suddenly it was over and he came home to the house in town and the bars by the railroad tracks and a night or two in jail and endless pieces of paper and then that too was over, the scar tissue thick over the past.

Suddenly he knew that it was. It was as dead and gone and meaningless after more than forty-five years as great-great grandfather John Q. and great-great grandmother Emily and great uncle John A. and those in the graves, named and nameless, here and in town. And he had a task to complete and then he would go. He put out the cigarette and walked back to the grave. He fixed the stone firmly, prying it up, bracing it, digging out the soft earth, and then pouring in the gravel. He leveled it carefully. He would not come this way again. He looked around, picked up a bit of sandstone with an indecipherable date and put it in his pocket. He carried the tools and the bucket back to the car, threw them in the trunk, closed it, and without looking back, he drove off. The gull still circled aimlessly overhead.

He would drive back to town, spend a silent Christmas alone with his mother in the old house built by his Irish grandfather with his first wartime profits and then he would drive through the towns of the past, through what had been Pittsfield, obliterated by a tornado, only the Civil War monument facing South in the pasture that once had been Elm Grove; through Birmingham, seedy but surviving; through now suburban Wellington, its past stylishly preserved, with its town hall restored and the clock striking the hours again after decades of silence; past the graveyards that held forgotten family connections. He would come onto the turnpike at Elyria and drive East at seventy-five miles an hour.

He had not exorcised the past nor obliterated it nor did he understand it. But it was. And the nearly three hundred pages ahead of him like those he had written so much earlier were wrong and he would burn them, too. The past was, but it had become usable, as controlled as the historical past that he used in his work. And there was the present and the face that haunted him was in the dead past, and it was no longer torturing or tortured. After almost half a century, it simply was. The pain in his shoulder was again a dull ache as he drove home knowing and yet not really caring what was between him and the end.

BEER THAT WE DRANK, LIES THAT WE TOLD

Last night was my first evening in town and vaguely on the town in more than thirty-five years. I left the hospital after visiting my mother just after eight and walked up my Midwestern Broadway. It was a Thursday in late October, and in the distance I could sense Lake Erie as the fresh breeze carried with it wafts of the musty, fishy smell that had characterized the lake for me as far into the past as I can remember; it smelled good after the laundered air of the hospital. I noted that empty stores, the grime, the occasional sleazy business, still open to catch the last furtive customer. Badly lit, it wasn't the Broadway I remembered, proudly proclaimed before the war to be "the longest boulevard-lighted street in the United States," nor was it the street where we used to park on summer Saturday nights in the thirties to watch the people and occasionally to buy a giant ice cream cone at Isaly's. Somehow, when Malraux removed the grime from Paris, I was offended; now I was more offended at the grime that had accumulated here in thirty-five years and the sleaziness that seemed institutionalized. I passed only a few people, saw perhaps a dozen cars.

Although my mother was doing well after her minor surgery -- at eight-five she was the matriarch her mother had been a generation before, and she wore the title energetically -- and I had felt reasonably content when I left the hospital, I became increasingly depressed and regretted that I hadn't driven the twenty or so blocks from my mother's house, where I had grown up. I was limping slightly, as I had for nearly forty years, and my right leg began its usual dull ache.

I hadn't walked twenty blocks in twenty years, and I regretted the sudden enthusiasm and curiosity that made me decide to do so.

At Nineteenth Street, the short block that ran East to the river, I turned, responding to another momentary surge of a cautious curiosity. Nineteenth was even more badly lit, but the sign I expected was still lit after two generations, as it had for a generation before. It was the local VFW post, named after two young men from the town who had died in France in 1918, and I remembered dimly the two old ladies who rode proudly in Memorial Day parades when I was a kid and believed in parades. I turned in and pushed the button above the door knob. It buzzed loudly, and I turned the knob and went in, as I hadn't since the Fall of 1947.

The barroom was as bright as I remembered it -- the younger members once attempted to romanticize the place by dimming the lights, I remembered, but the old timers resisted -- and I stood there a moment, letting my eyes adjust while I remembered. It hadn't changed much or I couldn't see any changes: the long bar along the wall at the left, the scattered tables, the doors to the restrooms and to the room that had once been lined with slot machines tightly closed, the latter now with a sign that said game room, the tables and chairs scattered haphazardly, a few booths along the wall to the right.

At the end of the bar was the sad, quiet man you see in every bar in the world, slowly, privately getting smashed, the television above him, but he didn't look up. At two or three tables pushed together a dozen or so young men, some bearded, some unshaven, some with long hair, were loudly drinking beer. The bartender, wiping his hands on his apron, looked at me as I walked over and sat down on a stool. I ordered a draft beer, and he nodded.

He looked about my age or a bit older, heavier, balder. I
didn't know him, but he could have been a clone of those I
remembered, remnants of their own war, who had stood
behind that bar in 1946. They liked to be called stewards, and
it was popularly believed that they had a good thing going,
diverting a percentage of the take to their pockets and
knowing when the slots would hit.

"You a member?" he asked as he put the beer down.

"I used to be, a long time ago." I paid him.

"You oughtta join again." He wiped his hands again.

"I don't live in town." I took a sip. The beer hadn't
changed either.

"We got lots of outa town members."

"Oh." Then: "Don't I know you?"

We exchanged names, shook hands. His was vaguely
familiar to me, but he didn't recognize mine, although my
father's name was on the charter on the wall, behind him, and
mine had become modestly well-known, occasionally noticed
by local columnists in the hometown paper. It wasn't exactly
a topic of barroom conversation, however, even in the student
bars two thousand miles away.

We talked desultory for a few minutes about the weather --
kind of nice for the end of October; the pro football strike --
greedy players, greedy owners, the fans are the suckers -- ;
the space shot that morning -- it's become a routine. I didn't
want to talk, however casually, but I didn't want not to.
Behind me the young men shouted for another round of beer.

As he set them up I decided to drink up and get out.
Drinking, I turned on the stool, looking first at the inane
game show on the television, the screen flickering, the sound

barely audible, and then at the man who sat there beneath it. Heavy, wearing a plaid jacket, his dirty gray hair uncombed, he seemed oddly familiar, and I remembered another quiet man getting privately smashed at the end of that bar thirty-five years before. I couldn't remember his name, but he had to be in his grave or in the Old Soldiers' Home in Sandusky. This could be his son.

The bartender came back and noticed that I was staring at the man, although I wasn't really aware that I was.

"That's old Oscar Tremaine. He's been sitting there since I got the job in 1961."

I remembered the name and said so, but I remembered more than I said: the red hair, the freckles, the incoherent chatter when he was loaded, his helplessness at closing time, midnight during the week, 2AM on weekends.

"He don't bother anybody. Just sits there and drinks up his seventy percent disability."

"I knew him when it was thirty."

"Before his liver went bad."

"I suppose."

"Some of the kids who come in used to ride him a bit." He gestured vaguely at the table behind me, where the voices were louder, the laughter shriller, the words more obscene. "But he didn't pay much attention and now they let him alone. He don't bother anybody," he said again, taking a swipe at the bar. "Maybe he'd remember you."

"Maybe." I finished my beer.

"But I doubt it." He reached down, pulled out a bottle of Schlitz and opened it. "Welcome back," he said grinning as he put it in front of me. I remembered how casually the bartender gave house drinks to the regulars.

"Thanks," I said. He waved in reply and then the bell rang. He reached under the bar to open the door, and it buzzed loudly. Neither Tremaine nor I looked around, but the young men began to shout the words that I remembered passed for welcome, for a diversion, for those who belonged, when they had probably seen last at closing time twenty hours before.

"Well, look who's here."

"Here comes the shit head."

"Hello, shit for brains."

"Ya gettin any?"

I knew the words, and I knew the vocabulary, but I hadn't heard either for a long time, nor did I want to now. But my only option was to leave, and again I decided to finish my beer. The doorbell rang again, the bartender passed in front of me to open it, two older men wearing work clothes and tan jackets sat down between me and Oscar Tremaine; the noise behind me got louder, and I wished I had walked on up Broadway to the Loop and home along the lake. But I hadn't, and I began to remember when, like the young men behind me, we drank beer and we talked about sex and the war at, I was sure, the very same tables in the same hard light that was, perhaps, as conducive to memory as it wasn't to romance.

The Civil War was no longer the central fact in the American experience in 1946 in spite of the words of lank desiccated Miss Frank in the high school on the hill of our youth, nor was the war of our fathers that had fascinated us so much when we were kids, and we ignored the old men who sat at the bar, those who had fought the war to end wars.

Our war was *the* war, as it always would be, and we laughed at the old men who wanted to talk about theirs, the old men who were younger than I was now. And somehow I rarely talked about our war any more, although it was never far below the surface of my mind.

Already, however, in early 1946, no more than weeks or months after we came home, sitting around in dirty khakis, in brightly-dyed OD shirts, in field jackets and loafers, we had begun to reorder that experience, to try to make it mean, as it already had been and had begun to recede. We talked about war and about sex, or about sex and about war, the two fused in our minds as landings made, battles fought, booze drunk, doses caught, as the young men behind me might joke about AIDS or herpes or dope.

The bartender was talking to the men down the bar; they glanced in my direction; I looked at my beer, remembering what we had said -- the sense rather than the sound or the words -- as we tried to force our reality to coincide with the self-image we sought, as heroes, as lovers, as clowns, as men, and we tried to absolve ourselves of the fear, the ignoble acts, the grimy sex, the trivia that had consumed so much of our youth.

It was fashionable among us to be the live coward, the survivor who, shit-scared or scared shitless, had somehow taken good care of number one. None of us -- the numbers fluctuated from two or three in the mornings to a dozen or more in the evenings -- had been friends before the war, although we had known or known of each other before, but now we were close, each of us aware of the violence that seethed just below the surface, that broke through in sudden bursts and flying fists, chairs upset, and the mumbled apologies that spelled out our need for each other.

218

In each of the stories the narrator was drunk or shit-scared or scared shitless, depending on the needs of the narrative and the mood of the moment, and each story made clear a bumbling heroism, a manhood devoid of all sentiment, a brief victory in the long skirmish with the system, each of us finally going for broke in his own preferred way.

Oscar Tremaine never had much to say as he drank beer after beer in single-minded devotion, but my stories were always well received, carefully plotted for a laugh. Sometimes I told them by special request, especially when one or more of us had brought along a chick and needed support in igniting a fire, a fire that rarely became flame except in drunken moments in the cramped back seats of the cars that we drove, that we rarely owned because the used car salesmen laughed at our need and our lack of jalopies to trade in.

Of the stories I told I remember three, none of which happened the way it was told. There was the time, in a drunken evening in Palermo, when I threw a whore's clothes out her third story window and then stood at the top of the stairs, pissing a stream and shouting "Niagara Falls!" until the MPs came; the time on the beachhead I called down artillery fire on an enemy latrine and laughed as three Krauts scurried for cover, their asses shining and running; the time in Southern France when we captured a Luftwaffe rest camp in a villa overlooking the sea, and the whores and the wine kept us from taking our objective until the next day.

Each of us knew the other's stories so well that sometimes we joined in shouting the punch line together. But each of us knew intuitively the stories we didn't tell, and the violence that sometimes erupted meant that a wound, barely healed, had been rubbed raw. Most of the time we managed to avoid the wounds just as we deliberately avoided the stories that had made them, and yet the truth was always there, crowded among us around the littered tables, drifting freely in the smoke and the lies.

The people around me then had not been my friends before the war, but I had dropped out of my crowd -- and some of us actually called it that -- when I enlisted. In 1946, in spite of my parents' protest, I had friends, and whatever it was that I was supposed to become had become, like Luckey Strike Green, a casuality of war, a casualty I didn't miss, nor have I yet.

Rarely, almost always in the mornings, we talked about what we would do, often about re-enlisting, and some of us did before the year was out, and they came home soberly trim, to unmerciful laughter. Gradually others drifted off, to jobs or to love, or back to wives they had neglected. One shot himself; another totaled his car and himself. And finally I drifted off too, late in 1947, and now I was back, alone, an old guy at the bar. I emptied my glass and began to get up.

The bartender and one of the men down the bar began to walk toward me, and I paused. The man, freshly shaved, greying hair thin but combed firmly back, grinned and stuck out his hand, and I knew who he was, one of those who had drifted off to find love or money sometime in that funny, pathetic, sad year.

He called me by a nickname I hadn't heard in years and I called him by his. We shook hands, grinned at each other, sat down and had another beer. We talked about how it had been, and I saw that behind the grin he was old. We talked about what we had done, he at length about the changes in the mill that fed the town, I, more reluctantly, but I hope not condescendingly, about what I was doing. His friend came over; we were introduced; I had once known him slightly, but he was a bit younger, an occupation vet. We laughed at what we had been, and once, briefly, at the noisy young men behind us. And then they had to go -- both were working 11 to 7, both would have their thirty-five years in in a few months, and both would be glad to retire, to fish and fuck, as one said laughingly, in the way it once had been. And then I walked out with them to their car and waved them off. I walked, limping a bit, down a grimy Broadway and along the misty lake toward home and an empty house. I read a while and was asleep before twelve.

IN THE CITY OF THE YOUNG

Nearly half a century before, at the end of one war, he had sat on the same stone bench beside the Roman Catholic cathedral in Novi Sad and looked across the rubble-strewn square at the heroic bronze sculpture of some minor despot as he waited for something that he knew could never happen. Then, in 1945, the cathedral was roofless, the city hall battered, the people ragged and hungry, only the despot triumphant.

As he sat there, his nearly healed legs ached, and he knew that it was over, that in a moment he would go, find a lift to Belgrade, and present himself to Allied Air Transport for a flight back to Naples and to a future he could not imagine.

He had come to Novi Sad the day before because he had to, because he said he would, because somewhere in the hills across the Danube, in the shadow of a gutted monastery he and the others had buried her.

And now in the Fall of 1990, as the clouds of another war gathered on the horizon beyond those hills he had again come to Novi Sad because he had to and because he knew that it would be for the last time.

In a moment he would go, as he had in the Spring of 1945, at the end of his war. Then he had left his youth behind in what was becoming the Serbian Socialist Republic; now it was at the end of a life as well as the beginning of a new war.

Novi Sad in 1990 was a city no longer in rubble but justly proud of its rebirth as a city of culture -- the white, modern Serbian National Theatre replaced the rubble that had dominated the north side of the square -- of learning -- the

University, new since the war, where he had come to lecture, was doggedly in pursuit of distinction and threatened to achieve it if it survived the shadow on the horizon, and above all, in 1990 as in 1945, it was a city of the young, of the throngs in the square, then and now, and of the youth, his own, lost at that fateful road junction, and hers, buried in the hills beyond the Danube for nearly fifty years. In a moment he would go, return briefly to the hotel, and then taxi to the airport at Belgrade and board the JAT flight for New York.

The night before he had lectured in Belgrade and had been greeted by the President of Serbia, as a distinguished visiting American professor and -- he thought it was odd that he had remembered it -- as what the President called a hero of the War of National Liberation. And then the post-lecture reception ebbed and flowed, a quartet played, a soprano sang, and as his hosts drove him back to Novi Sad, he sensed that what Wilson and Versailles had united in an arbitrary order, what Tito and Mihailovic had fought over, what Tito had captured and, supported by Churchill and Stalin, and, oddly, he, himself, had reaffirmed, was coming apart, had become as redundant as the Warsaw Pact and NATO, even as redundant as the Soviet Union that was itself disintegrating.

For a moment, thinking in the impersonality of geopolitical terms, in the jargon of his profession, had taken him out of himself, out of the square and what had once been; memories phrased in the language of the lecture hall distanced himself not only from two generations of students who had sat in front of him, but from the memories themselves. And yet they were there, buried beneath the psychic scar tissue of pain and time and youth buried under an oak tree in the hills beyond the Danube.

His participation in what was for Yugoslavia simultaneously a war of liberation and one of the many wars to determine the next phase of its future was as brief as his heroism, so generously lauded the night before, was minor. He had come to Yugoslavia at 19, in mid-September of 1943, little more than a year out of high school in that part of Ohio, that still thought proudly of itself as the Firelands, out of the ashes of that long-ago war that had made the United States a nation. But he had come too out of the fate that made him not an expert eighteen-year-old infantryman or a flyboy or a clerk in a Virginia warehouse but the chance and foolishness that made him volunteer for demolition work, that had sent him to Tunisia and then across the beaches at Gela, Sicily, and at Salerno, and then to something called the Inter-Allied Commando and Yugoslavia and finally, early in January, 1944, back to Italy and Anzio and the long stay in the hospital in Naples. But in little more than three months in Yugoslavia he had fought the most intense war of his career and had become what had been called a hero of the War of National Liberation and he had rediscovered his youth and then had buried it with her under an oak tree in the Serbian hills of Vojvodina, beyond the Danube.

He had come to Yugoslavia to teach the Chetniks under General Draza Mihailovic to use new American explosive ordinance to best effect in destroying German supply lines by river, rail, and road from Hungary to the Adriatic, an assignment that seemed to promise little more than an interesting interlude in a part of the world his high school history courses had mentioned only in passing and about which neither he nor the commanding officer who selected him knew anything except that somehow it was a backwater of war, where nothing important was possible. And he was given a code name that had vanished from his memory, had gone, by British ML, from Taranto and across the Adriatic to a rocky inlet south of Split and the momentary intensity of ME109 strafing as, with a British Lieutenant-Colonel and a courtly civilian guide of indeterminate nationality, he disappeared into the brush, moving in a direction vaguely East.

And in three months he had found not a backwater nor a respite but the most brutal and bloody of wars and he had met her -- he still could not think of her as Code Name Anna, the only name by which he had known her -- as a member of the Chetnik battalion which he officially advised and unofficially led in the short time before he buried her in the hills and had sought and been denied a grave of his own by the vagaries of chance and the betrayal unfolding in far-off Cairo and of which he would remain unaware for nearly thirty years.

The war in Yugoslavia, like those he had known in Tunisia and Sicily and Italy was small in scope and intensely personal. The battalion he was to train was that in name only; it could rarely marshal a company-sized group; it was heavy in rank and age, with a small number of women. Most were Serbians, a few were Croatians, Montenegrins, Hungarians; all shared a mild devotion to the monarchy, to the Federation, and the young King in far off London; what truly united them was the intensity of their hatred of the Germans, the ferocity of their courage, and the stoicism with which they shed their blood and gave up their lives in the countless forgotten raids, ambushes, and assaults that made up their war and that quickly became his.

At some time soon after the courtly guide and the British half-colonel introduced him to the battalion commander, a Serb called Code Name Radovic, gave up their share of the plastic explosive that each of the three of them had carried into the mountains, and vanished into the brush, he became aware of the lack of direction of the unit, the carelessness with which lives and materiel were expended on useless hillsides and meaningless road junctions in firefights that had no purpose but to kill Germans at whatever cost in Chetnik lives became necessary, and he became aware too of his almost total inability to communicate with the battalion, much less to instruct or to give a measure of purpose to what seemed to him a great deal of courageously misguided effort.

He knew no Serbo-Croatian, but Radovic and a few others knew a bit of basic English, and so they did a great deal of smiling and grunting and shaking hands. And then he became aware of a young woman, one of six in the battalion, who introduced herself as Code Name Anna. She seemed perhaps twenty-five; she had a vague staff rank, and she was fluent in English -- and, he later learned, in French, German, and Hungarian as well as her own Serbo-Croatian.

And somehow, from that moment, he began to feel part of the unit, to feel, indeed to share in, the beat of its pulse, and to find some measure of strength in himself to match theirs. And slowly they became a functioning unit with Anna -- Code Name Anna -- at its heart as through her he taught them what he knew -- not about explosives; they had almost none except outmoded fuseless air bombs for tactical purposes, much less instruction, but about roadblocks, about ambushes, about raids, about aggressive but controlled attacks, about strategic retreats, about lines of communication, however primitive, and about the value of lives expended for cause and at high cost to the enemy.

And he learned -- mostly about the vagaries of Yugoslavian politics, about the aborted efforts of Chetniks --

royalists -- and Partisans -- Communists -- to work together and the growing enmity between them and the accusations made by and about each group. And he learned, too, that many of these contemporary quarrels and hatreds among Serbians, Croatians, Slovenians, Montenegrins, and what were called Turks were extensions of what had begun in the Middle Ages and before, and that no war or peace could ever end.

Their war was truly a guerrilla war, based loosely in the small towns and villages where Serbia and Bosnia met, along the river Sava, a war of small unit actions and rapid movements and deaths that could not be replaced and wounded who were left behind, at the mercy of peasant women in isolated farmhouses, to recover or not, and they were rarely aware of which it was. The fall and early winter passed rapidly and dragged endlessly.

And during those days he came to know Anna and she, hopelessly young, infinitely wise, total in her dedication, became part of him. She was not twenty-five, but twenty-two, a Serb, Orthodox, a mild Royalist, a fervent nationalist; she was from Novi Sad, a city on the Danube; her father, an academic, and her mother were killed in one of the earliest German raids, and she, an only child, had become a Chetnik.

When the war was over, when Yugoslavia was free and Peter sat on the throne of his father she would return to Novi Sad and discover her life; until then, her dedication was complete. At least two of the young officers, perhaps even Radovic himself, were devoted to her, but to her they were instruments to be manipulated for the cause, to be expended, if necessary, or traded for the lives of Germans on the most favorable terms possible. During his first month with the battalion, training and tactical action were one, directed by what intelligence could be gathered from the locals, from peasants to clergy, and from rare directives from Mihailovic's headquarters, from occasional communiques from Inter-Allied Commando, and from their almost constant scouting, listening, and probing. Their strategic assignment was the disruption of German supply lines; their tactical mission was to use whatever means they could; their battles remained as nameless as they were minor; their troops were all volunteer of the loosest kind, their loyalties more often to a village or a piece of countryside, and their service as limited.

Radovic, Anna, and he became a unit in which they shared experience, instinct, and what they knew about the situation and their always limited ability to control it. But their determination to do what they could, and Anna's hatred for the Germans and her determination to destroy them had, he learned, one tempering factor: her compassion for the peasants and villagers, who always, she kept pointing out, not only paid for this war, as they had for every war since time began, but they paid too for the battalion's own small scale operations.

German armor controlled the roads by day as the Luftwaffe did the air, and the troop carriers they ambushed, the bridges they blew, the stragglers they caught and banished to the hands of a nearby Partisan unit could never affect the course of the war. He remembered clearly the moment when her passions clashed in a rare instant when her control slipped.

They had caught a German platoon-sized motor patrol crossing the Sava on a bridge they had partially blown the week before with the captured Czech explosives that were always less than reliable; the combination of captured Schmeisser machine guns, pre-war Yugoslavian Mausers, British Stens, and his own GI Thompson caught them by surprise; the first vehicles crashed on the bridge, and those following piled up as they tried to make misdirected turns, and some went down the steep bank into the river. When they withdrew, seven vehicles were destroyed, one was captured, and perhaps three escaped. German dead and wounded were left behind uncounted; the battalion took eleven prisoners and faded into the brush toward a rendezvous point at an old mill where a stream came rushing out of the living rock. That evening, secure, he walked along the stream, wondering at the force that drove it.

He came upon Anna, sitting on a rock, her feet in the water, toweling her freshly-washed hair. He watched for a moment, marveling at the innocence of the scene, the contrast with what had transpired a few hours before, the vigor with which she transmitted orders and reports as she moved from language to language, matched by the vigor with which she dried her hair, and yet a scene that denied the very existence of Code Name Anna, her war, and her dedication to something that could not exist in that moment. She sensed his approach and turned. She looked impossibly young, and for a moment they simply looked at each other, her dark eyes wide.

"I'm sorry. I didn't mean to interrupt you," he said.

"It's no interruption. I've finished what I had to do."

"Your hair is lovely. I had no idea."

"Perhaps it should remain under that old cap. But I couldn't resist the chance to wash it in that water. It's so clean, so pure. And downstream in the Sava . . ."

He knew what she meant. "At least it's clean and pure for the moment." Then: "And for this moment your hair is as free and clean and pure as the river." He smiled, drawn to her, sensing that the encounter was touching something he hadn't expected and wasn't sure he should pursue. Then, without thinking, "You're a very lovely woman, Anna. You belong in such a setting, if only for the moment."

"And the moment is just that. And then again we must kill. And they kill us. And the villagers are shot for helping us or for helping them. And the Partisans hate us and we them. And there is no end to the madness, the killing." She looked down at her feet in the water.

"But the war will end."

"Yes. It ended for those Germans today. And tonight for the villagers in retaliation."

"No. It'll end for us—for everybody -- and we can go on. You'll go back to Novi Sad . . . "

"What do you know? You Americans will go home and we'll try to rebuild for the next war."

"No. You'll go to Novi Sad and I'll come there and we'll know the war is over."

"It is nice to think so. That our war will end, that we can sit in the square in Novi Sad, and watch the sun set beyond the hills."

"It will come."

"It is nice to think so." She shook her head, and a few drops of water sprinkled his face. She rose, stepped out of the stream, and smiled quickly. "And now our interlude is over, my hair is nearly dry, and my feet are cold. And tomorrow is another war." She walked back to the camp by the mill, and he followed, sensing that somehow, for a moment, they had touched something in each other, that perhaps other moments like it might occur.

And they did, on occasion, in the next several weeks, and they began to talk quietly of Novi Sad in some spring almost within reach, and, although they rarely touched and never talked about a relationship real or imaged or hoped for, he sensed that one might emerge, and he knew that she did too. But first there was the war.

At the end of November the battalion was ordered to join forces with four others, two Chetnik and two Partisan, in one of the first coordinated attacks of the resistance, upon a supply depot in the town of Sabac on the Sava, a major German supply point protected by a sizable garrison. Radovic was delighted.

Anna was apprehensive but determined; he was convinced that it could be done, that it marked an important change in the direction of the war. They inspected the arms, distributed ammunition, hoped that the supporting artillery -- Russian pack howitzers carried and manned by Partisans, a new dimension in the war -- would be effective.

The battalion would lead the assault; he and Radovic and Anna poised over drawings and maps, questioned troops and civilians from the area. And yet Anna was somber, her lips occasionally moving, in what he was convinced was prayer. Somehow, he knew, something had happened to her in the past several weeks, and he knew that it had happened also to him.

The attack was designed to be a major strategic and tactical turning point for the war in central Yugoslavia; it would mark the transition from a guerrilla war to a war of competing armies; it would mark the beginning of close cooperation between Chetniks and Partisans; it would send a clear message to the German-supported Croatian republic through the local troops the German had conscripted; it

232

would justify and encourage greater allied support. And from the beginning something went terribly, terribly wrong.

In late afternoon as the assaulting group moved up through the brush to the edge of town, the four-gun battery fired one salvo -- four rounds -- that fell short of the targeted buildings and then, as the battalion, at its maximum strength of almost two hundred men and women, began its advance, German mortars -- unreported by intelligence -- began counter-battery fire and then dropped onto the assault wave.

Radovic signaled the battalion to take cover and then, as the mortar fire ceased, to advance again. They hoped desperately for the artillery support, but none came. Radovic and the two flanking battalions, totaling about two-company strength, tried to coordinate a desperate assault, but the mortars fired again in clusters punctuating the rapid fire of Schmeissers.

The assault team began to shout and to fire at random at an enemy that still couldn't be seen, and then they sought cover to regroup. Dead and wounded littered the slope as the mortars fell still.

For a moment Radovic and he pondered another assault. But the flanking battalions were silent, and the low moans of the wounded, punctuated by a single long scream, echoed in the silence. Radovic shook his head, looked to his flanks and then shrugged his shoulders. There was nowhere to go except the inevitable, and he and Radovic signaled the withdrawal.

Suddenly he saw Anna, a hundred yards away, scramble to her knees, and he shouted to her to take cover, to crawl back, and as she turned he saw that she was crying and then a Schmeisser fired and she clutched her chest and fell and was still. He got up to run to her and the mortars began again and the Schmeissers and there was nothing to do but take cover and wait until dark.

At dusk they began their withdrawal, and he and Radovic went forward to carry Anna back. There was a small hole in the middle of her chest, a larger exit wound, and comparatively little blood. She was surprisingly light. Her cap fell off in the brush and her hair fell free as they carried her through the night.

At dawn they came on the ruins of a monastery, and they dug a shallow grave in its shadow, under a giant oak. He covered her face and her hair with his jacket and turned away as Radovic and the others began to cover her with the moist soil. And then it was over, and they went on, deeper into the hills.

Whatever went wrong he never knew, but the assault had been clearly doomed from the start, and there was nothing they could do. Stunned, decimated, Anna's absence like a hole in their hearts, the unit began to fall apart.

For weeks he was numb, and then a messenger came. He was withdrawn from the battalion, he would accompany the messenger to the coast and return to Italy for reassignment. South of Split he met others, British and Americans, who were also withdrawn from Chetnik units. It was the time of the betrayal of the Loyalist Chetniks in far-off Cairo and Tito's political triumph, but none of them knew it.

As he boarded the ML at dusk for the run across the Adriatic, he knew that his real war, much of his life, was over.

Somehow, still numb, he had returned to his unit in Italy, decimated by its weeks in the mountains around Cassino, and then, at Anzio, he caught what had eluded him in the hills, in the ambushes, in the failed massive assault. But he lived and came to Novi Sad at the end of his war and again after nearly half a century, and he sat on the bench as he had so many years before, and he looked across the square at the statue of the despot and at the young people who gathered there on the eve of a new war, of their war. And then the moment was over, lost in all the other moments that make up the past, and he walked back toward the hotel on his way back toward what he called home.

About the Author

David D. Anderson, University Distinguished Professor at Michigan State University, is author or editor of thirty-six books and more than three hundred articles, essays, short stories, and poems. A native Ohioan and a veteran of both World War II and the Korean War, he has received the Michigan State University Book Manuscript Award for his critical biography SHERWOOD ANDERSON, MSU's Distinguished Faculty Award, Bowling Green State University's Distinguished Alumnus Award, the Society for the Study of Midwestern Literature's Distinguished Service Award, and the honorary degree of Litt. D. from Wittenberg University. He edits MidAmerica, Midwestern Miscellany, and SSML Newsletter, and has lectured throughout Europe, Asia, and Australia. He is listed in WHO'S WHO IN THE WORLD, WHO'S WHO IN AMERICA, and other sources.

COLLEGE OF ARTS AND LETTERS
DEPARTMENT OF AMERICAN
THOUGHT AND LANGUAGE

EAST LANSING • MICHIGAN • 48824-1033

July 4, 1998

Dear Paul:

With your abiding interest
in World War II you may
be interested in the enclosed.
Some of the stories are old —
shortly after the war — and some
are new. I hope you like them.

Cheers,

Dave Anderson